Advance Praise for
Somewhere Between the Trees and Clouds

"*Somewhere Between the Trees and Clouds* is heartfelt, heart-breaking, and heart-full. This beautiful, necessary novel in verse deals with some tough subjects—abuse and mental health—but does so with insight, tenderness, honesty, and hope."

—Jennifer Niven, #1 *New York Times* bestselling author of *All the Bright Places*

"Chuck Murphree has fashioned a creative storytelling vehicle that is captivating, and he tells a story that is deeply touching and engaging. This book will bring understanding and validation to teens and adults struggling with powerful life events in a way that is real, compassionate, and healing."

—Scott A. Ritchie, Ph.D., clinical and consulting psychologist

"Chuck Murphree has created an important, accessible work that will speak to many teens facing one or more of the adversities contained within . . . Readers who see themselves or a loved one reflected in the story will find comfort, perhaps encouragement. Others may find this to be a window into understanding those whose challenges they do not know. The free verse form of *Somewhere Between the Trees and Clouds* allows the reader to connect deeply with the many painful experiences shared while not being distracted or bogged down in the overdevelopment which might have existed in a more traditional prose format. Highly recommended for HS library collections and perhaps for use in counseling/support group environments."

—Val Edwards, MLS, NBPT, educational consultant

"I would easily give this book 5 stars. I love how Murphree uses his writing talent to raise awareness of mental health issues that so many people unfortunately face. This book (like his first) is very powerful . . . It's a book that shows people that there can be hope even in the darkest of times. That no matter how bad things get, there are still good people out there who will want to help you to never give up."

—Samantha Atkins, author of *The Wing Thief*

"The power of words. The power of these words is found in *Somewhere Between the Trees and Clouds*, and the power of words are those that Dylan, a high school senior, uses to heal. This beautifully constructed novel in verse brings awareness and insight to mental health and the aftermath of rape . . . The story informs, heals, and offers hope."

—Teresa Voss, high school librarian

"Through poetic verse that cascades off the page, Murphree's *Somewhere Between the Trees and Clouds* takes the reader deep into the soul of 17-year-old Dylan. As Dylan claws through his final year of high school, he lives with old and faces new tragedies that threaten his graduation, his dreams, and his life. With the unflinching support of his family and best friend, and with the emergence of new love, he struggles for the strength to move forward. By the end of the story, Dylan forges a path that not every reader has taken, but the journey is one that impacts each of us. Along the way, every character who Dylan touches, and every reader who finishes the story, is better for it."

—Gary M. Arnold, program director of Progress Center for Independent Living (Forest Park, IL) and former president of Little People of America

"As an English teacher, I'm excited to add this novel-in-verse to my classroom library . . . Murphree's voice is raw and authentic. Students will be pulled into the deep emotions of grief and shame, but also revived by the power of family and friendship. What an extremely important topic to share with young adults."

—Emily Waisanen, English teacher and author of the children's book *The Book Monster*

"Emotional and Real. *Somewhere Between the Trees and Clouds* opens up emotions that are honest and hidden, in a way so real and telling that my eyes were opened up to so much outside my daily life. As a teacher, you do not know the background of every child. Chuck Murphree tells a story that is more real then we all like to think and affects more children then seems imaginable. Thank you, Chuck, for being vulnerable to share this story and open the eyes of your readers."

—Lauren Guelig, teacher and author of *Wish Me A Rainbow*

"Written by a man about a teenage boy, *Somewhere Between the Trees and Clouds* uniquely addresses the sensitive and often avoided issue of sexual abuse. Author Chuck Murphree draws the reader into the world of his complex characters through his concise prose. Even though he writes about a hard subject, it is an easy read that will have you quickly engaged and invested in the story."

—Marla Perfect, bilingual author, translator, former kindergarten teacher, and full-time mom

Somewhere Between the Trees and Clouds

CHUCK MURPHREE

Ten | 16
PRESS

www.ten16press.com - Waukesha, WI

Somewhere Between the Trees and Clouds
Copyright © 2022 Chuck Murphree
ISBN 9781645383512
First Edition

Somewhere Between the Trees and Clouds
by Chuck Murphree

For information, please contact:

www.ten16press.com
Waukesha, WI

Cover designer: Kaeley Dunteman
Editor: Lauren Blue

Dedication:

This book is for Karen, who came along when I needed to feel something different, magical, a love that has lasted since we were fifteen. Our life is a beautiful song with lyrics that have been written in stone.

To Mom, you are the reason for a boy's survival. Your breath is now fading, and I feel it wholly, within my soul, but what brings me grace is knowing that we will unite again one day and share laughter in a place of peace and healing.

In memory of Hazel, the sweetest of dogs.

ONE

There are two doors to this office,
One comes in from Student Services,
The other
Only God knows.
I feel like it's about to open up,
Swallow me and
My youth.
Will it come and take me
Away
To a basement where
Troubled kids go?
Students talk about that door.
It seems nothing is on the other side.
Abyss.
No hallway.
Just wall and it
Ends.
Everything ends
I suppose.

I say, "It was only weed."
But the cop doesn't look at me.
I say, "It was my first time."
But the dean looks like he's about
To vomit for some reason.
Then silence.

My only defense
Is not to say anything.
I fight my mouth and my stomach
Not to throw up.

The dean takes notes.
The cop scratches his
Clean-shaven face.
I clench my fist until my
Knuckles turn white.
The phone rings.
"Send him in," says the dean.
"Who in?" I don't even know
What I just said,
My voice sounds in my head
Like it's underwater.
Garbled.
That's my mind,
Drowning.

I sit back and wait.
"Who's coming?"
I say nervously,
A little more clear.
The dean looks down.
The cop drops his head.
"It's only weed,"
I say one more time.

Why did I hand it over?
Stupid.
Nervous.
I suck!
Did I say stupid?
Maybe idiot is a better word.

My palms are sweaty.
The dean leaves.
The door is wide open.
The other door,
The abyss,
Is still closed.

The cop smiles
A slanted grin,
Trying to offer comfort
Without saying a word.
I'm not buying it.
"It's only weed!" I plead.

I could run.
I think about it.
They would never catch me.
I'm fast,
Though the cop looks fast.
Slim and strong.
He must skip the donuts.
His gun would drag him down,
Steel security on his side.

Would he even try to chase me?
Doubtful,
Since it was only weed.

I ease closer
To the edge of my seat,
Glancing down.
My shoes are tied.
The door closes.
The dean is back
With my brother.
"Dylan," says Peter,
Happy to see me.
And then, "What did you do?"
His voice scolds me
As does his frown.
He's seen this before,
Me in trouble.
He's nineteen now,
Two years
My elder,
And he knows it.

"Nothing!" I exclaim.
Peter wouldn't know what weed is.
Peter has Down syndrome.
His hands are wrinkled from
Washing dishes
In his classroom.

He shakes his finger at me
In disapproval.
I almost smile,
But I always want
Peter's approval,
So I stop myself.

"Are you in trouble?"
Peter comes up and hugs me
Like he always does.
"No," I say. It was only..."
Silence.
No more confessions.

Peter looks at the cop.
"You arrest him?"
My defense attorney.
"He's a good guy."
Peter pats my shoulder.
"You should let him go.
He needs lunch."
Great defense.
The cop lowers his head,
Which makes me see flames
Because he's ignoring Peter.
Red, hot, fucking flames.
I grip my own hands.
White flesh rises
On bony fingers.

The dean says,
"Peter, you want some chips?"
Bribing my brother with food
Always works.
The dean is crafty.
He's getting Peter on his side.
He looks at me, the dean,
And then lowers his head.
Everyone is afraid of eye contact.
Damn, it was only weed.

He and the cop
Struggle
To look at my face.
Maybe they pity me
Because they know
Dad will be pissed
And Mom will be hurt,
And I'll be grounded for
A thousand years,
Or at least a month.

I should have never bought
The weed.
But my anxiety was
Torturous,
Leaving my mind shake
And my body tingle.
Intrusive thoughts
Tearing at my brain

And flesh.
I couldn't take it anymore
And needed to escape
Myself.

"It was only weed,"
I whisper to no one.
The cop raises his head.
The dean gives Peter
Three more high fives
As Peter thanks him for the chips
That he devours.

Crumbs fall all over Peter's shirt.
It turns orange from the chemicals,
Some sort of cheese seasoning
That's addictive
To every teenager,
Especially Peter.

"I need to use the bathroom," I say.
The dean looks up.
He sees my intentions
To escape and leave the building.
Would they really try to chase me?
It was only weed.

The dean motions
Towards the door
Where they must keep the bad kids.

I shake my head. "No."
The dean stands and
Moves toward the door.
He turns the knob.
This is it.
I want to yell at Peter to
Make a run for it.
The zombie teens will come out,
The ones that were
Sacrificed.
I'll be taken
To the bottom of this
Crummy institution,
Never to see daylight again,
Buried.
And then the door opens.

The bathroom is small.
A toilet and sink
With a poster of the Beatles
Walking across Abbey Road.
Not sure of the connection
The Beatles have with this
Black hole in the dean's office.
I walk through the opening,
Lock the door behind me,
And have to wonder in a whisper,
"Will my parents think it was only weed?"

I hear noise
Outside the bathroom door.
My fate awaits as I listen to
Dad's voice
Being drowned out by
Peter's enthusiasm to see him.
"Where's Dylan?" I hear Dad.
"In the bathroom," say the dean and Peter
At the same time,
Their voices oddly synchronous.
"What did he do now?" asks Peter.
"You should let him eat lunch." He's still
Pleading my release.
No one answers.

I slowly wash my hands,
Attempting to grab water.
It's a failed attempt.
Water just bends and flows.
I use the paper towel
To erase the wetness
and turn the knob.
I give one last look to
John, Paul, George, and Ringo,
And for a moment I think,
"Why is Ringo's name always
Mentioned last?"
He's cool.

I give John a nod and grin,
Knowing he'd think it
Was only weed.

Dad takes one look at me
And tears fill his eyes.
Peter hugs him like a bear.
I'm scared
And suddenly want to
Jump into the poster
And walk Abbey Road
Or sing "Sun King,"
My favorite.

Dad comes closer.
He's always been overly
Sensitive,
But it's cool
Because they are
His feelings,
Better than
No feelings,
Like some
That call themselves
"Father."
He looks me
Directly in the eye.
I caught up to him
This past summer,

Otherwise I'd be looking
Up.

His mouth comes
Closer to my ear.
Dad leans in.
I can feel his grip
Clench my skinny shoulders.
I smell his
Aftershave,
Old Spice,
The same I have been smelling
Since I was a kid
Because some things
Never change,
And that's good.
"She's dead,"
Dad whispers softly
And melts against me.

I'm motherless,
So now when TJ gives me shit
And says his favorite line,
"You motherless whore,"
He will be right.
That's what friends are for,
To give you shit.
Never understood that term.
And why is that my first thought?

Head spinning,
Dizzy,
An erosion of
Thought falls
Off my brain.

I can't cry,
I'm more dazed.
My eyes feel dry
Like the news has had the
Opposite effect
And closed up my tear ducts,
Stealing my saliva glands too
Because my mouth is
Suddenly parched.
No words can leave
Or even form.

Dad loosens his grip.
Peter comes into me,
And I feel like a
Sack of potatoes was tossed at me
From a fifty-foot building,
Smashing into my gut,
Stealing my breath.

Peter doesn't know yet why
Dad is crying
Or why
I lost my voice,

But he knows something is wrong
Because Peter has a
Better instinct about
Feelings
Than anyone I know.
Peter, my brother,
An empath.

There's a time
Before death
And a time after.
The world changes
In one heartbeat,
Or loss of a
Heartbeat,
And leaves you
Empty of
Everything.

The cop lowers his head.
The weed is gone.
I guess
It really was
Only weed.

The dean gives Peter more chips.
His hands are still orange from the last bag.
And then he hands me my backpack
Which he had gathered from
My Advanced Algebra class

Where I was called from
And happy about
Because algebra, I know,
Is of no use to me and never will be.
"I will contact all of your teachers and
Let them know
You will be gone,"
Says the dean as he gives me a
Gentle punch on the arm.
I don't know him and don't want to,
And I certainly don't want his sympathy
Or his "bro" punch.
What I want is my weed
And to escape this fucking place
And go see my mother's dead body
And...
I don't know what the fuck I want
Because I'm now spinning
On a merry-go-round
In my mind,
Trying to see if there
Is a safe place to jump off.

My anxiety is emerging
Panic!
My breathing becomes rapid
Panic!
I try to fight it
Panic!
It doesn't let go

Panic!
I'm breathing fast and suffocating all at once
Attack!

Dad walks me through the
Breathing exercises
That the therapist taught me
And the yoga teacher that Mom
Sent me to.
"Therapy for your mind,
Running for your body,
And yoga for both," Mom would say.
I always thought maybe it was because
I was both crazy and weak.
Mom didn't like it when I said that,
CRAZY and WEAK,
To describe myself,
My illness,
and I want to say it now.
Scream it!
To see if somehow she would hear it
And it would bring her back
To tell me I was
Magnificent and Unique,
Because those are the two words
Mom always used to
Describe me.
"You are magnificent, Dylan."
And she would kiss my right cheek.
"You are unique, Dylan."

And she would kiss my left cheek.
But I can't talk because
I'm having a fucking
Panic attack.
Breathless.

We exit the dean's office,
Walk through the line of kids
Waiting to see a counselor
Or the social worker.
Their faces a blur
As I pass,
Head still spinning,
And we leave the building
Where I have never felt included,
Normal,
And I wonder if I will ever
Have to return.

TWO

Dad drives,
Peter sits next to him,
Reading the street signs.
I'm in back,
Head out the window
A quarter of the way.
Wind blowing my hair,
Wind blowing my tears,
Wind blowing my pain,
Wind blowing my grief,
Wind blowing my anxiety,
Wind blowing my depression.
Begging the wind
To blow me away.

Dad says, "You need to get out, Dylan."
I say, "Where are we?" Not even realizing
The car has stopped.
My world has stopped.
"Home." He offers a hand,
The wrong hand.
I want Mom's hand,
The one I've held for
Seventeen years.
I weep.

Dad lets me stay in the car,
But not before
A hug
That only Dad can deliver.
It's fierce,
Like my spine is breaking.
Dad can be fierce
With his love for his sons.

I'm lifeless.
I'm exhausted.
I'm lost.
I'm wanting to die.
I want
To see her
One more time,
And tell her I love her
One more time,
To have
One more time,
One moment,
Since life is about
Moments.

Peter is next to me.
He is more forceful,
Taking my hand,
Pulling,
Prying.

"Get up," he says
And yanks on my hand.
"Come see Mom.
She's waiting."

My breath stops,
Mom!
I scream
In my head,
Mom!
I want her to hear me
Through my bellowing
Thoughts,
Mom!

I'm greeted at the door.
She sees me and cries,
Which surprises me.
Hospice nurses
Don't cry,
They console,
But Erin
Is different.
Witnessing
Lingering death,
Slowly dying,
As Mom has,
Brings strangers
Together.

Erin takes my hand.
I feel a false sense
Of comfort
From her touch.
Then I feel guilty
For thinking what
I thought,
Teenage boy fantasies,
And then Erin guides me to
My mother.
Dead.
Lifeless.
Pale.
But now she's
Without pain.
I fall to my knees
And feel pain.
It shoots up through
My spine,
As if the floor
Punched through me.
I want it,
All of the pain my
Mom experienced.
I want to feel what she did.
Then I realize I am going
Numb
In my mind
Because the past few months
Pause all at once,

Leaving me without any
Thought
Except her
Pale face seemed
To have gained color after
Death.
How?

Mom is here
Before me.
I crawl to her
Like when I was a
Toddler
Except she doesn't
Reach out
To help me stand.
Her body
Still,
Lifeless.
Her face
Calm,
Painless.
Eyes closed,
Lips closed,
Gone.

I lift her hand
To my face
And kiss it,
Whispering, "I love you,"

Whispering, "Don't leave me,"
Whispering, "I need you...to survive,"
Whispering, "Goodbye."
My head falls onto her shoulder
Where I have lain since I was
A baby,
Seeking comfort
That only a mother can give.
She's gone.
Comfort gone.
I'm gone.

Peter says hello to Mom
Instead of
Goodbye,
Which is not odd for him,
But I wonder what he's
Thinking by giving a greeting
Instead of a farewell?

Dad kneels next to her.
"My darling, my life,
I will see you again one day,
But for now..."
He pauses and lays
His cheek against hers,
Kisses her forehead,
Looks back at his sons,
Leans in closer.
"I'm needed here, my love."

They take
Mom's body
Away
And drive down
The road
In the nicest car
She's ever ridden in.

I don't eat.
I don't talk.
I don't sleep.
I sit and stare.
I feel nothing.
I lied,
I feel Everything.

Morning comes and Peter gets ready for school.
Morning comes and I can't get up.
Morning comes and Dad says,
"Your brother wants to go to school. Take him, please."
Morning comes and Mom is gone
As I check her bedroom one more time
Where she has lain for weeks.
Was it real?
Then, "I can't take him to school. My car is at school."
Dad cries.
I cry.
The smallest of things make you cry
When your world is torn apart.

Peter hugs us both and says, "It'll be okay."
Consoling.

Peter knows more than most do
Emotionally.
He knows Mom is gone
But says he will see her again,
So he's okay.
Peter says, "I can talk to Mom whenever I want."
He reassures us both as he holds my head against Dad's,
Then we all start laughing because our skulls are crushing.
The pain feels good,
The pressure of being squeezed by love.
If only we were all like Peter.

Dad and I drop Peter off,
A teacher's assistant,
Karla,
Waits for him
To walk,
And hug,
And laugh,
And make him feel "normal,"
Like his mother didn't just die.
As Peter laughs, I wonder,
Will I get to talk to Mom like Peter?
Seems comforting,
Needed.

"Didn't Peter want to be there?" I ask.
"He said he wanted to work today," says Dad.
"He doesn't want to see Mom?"
"He said he saw her last night." Dad starts to cry.
I envy Peter
And then I cry with Dad.

The drive to the funeral home is
A mile away,
And I stare into the
September sky
And notice the leaves
Changing.
Everything changes,
Life changes
In a moment's notice.

The dress sways
From the hanger
As Dad carries it.
Purple.
I saw her wear it once
On Christmas Eve.
Mom doesn't wear dresses,
More like
Jeans, or maybe
Running shorts,
Yoga pants.
If you want to put her on
Fucking display,

Have her dressed right.
Mom would have laughed
At that thought
And been proud
That I kept it just a thought,
Deep
Inside,
Where most things remain.

Arrangements are made.
I don't remember any of it.
Dad and I get breakfast,
But neither of us can eat.
We laugh
At the plate of eggs
And side of pancakes
Staring at us
With what looks like
Bulging eyes.
The waitress says, "Anything else?"
As she frowns at sunny-side up eggs
Staring back at her
In full form.
Dad gives her a thirty-percent tip.
He feels bad we occupied space.
Isn't that what we all do daily
For our entire lives?
Occupy space?

THREE

I've been to one funeral,
Grandpa's.
His body was old,
Wrinkled,
Weathered,
Stiff,
And broken
From a war
That nobody wanted.
And they now have a wall
Full of names
To honor the dead.

Who will honor Mom?
We wait to view her,
Her three men.
View her?
I've viewed Mom ever since I've
Had eyes.

Fuck you, eyes.
Fuck you, ears.
Fuck you, mouth.
Fuck you, heart.
Fuck you, lungs.
Fuck...
You...

Breath...
Panic!

Dad rubs my back.
"Breathe deep, slowly," he coaches,
Trying to use Mom's tone,
Mom's method,
To calm me.
Peter puts his head
Against my shoulder.
His touch,
Peter's touch,
Brings me back
To normal.
Is there a
Normal
Anymore?

The funeral celebrant waits.
That's what he calls himself,
Celebrant.
What the fuck are we
Celebrating?
Again, Mom would have
Been proud
That I kept that thought
In my head.
"Please, come with me,"
The celebrant says,
As he sees I've calmed.

We walk.
My legs move,
I think, as
I look down,
Willing them to
Go forward.
No feeling.
Am I floating,
I wonder?
The walls pass me,
Suffocating me.
Peter guides me.
His arms are strong.
We approach.
"Mom!"
I scream,
I fall,
I cry,
I melt.

Peter lifts me.
Dad touches
Mom's hand.
Peter guides me
Closer.
"She told me to
Watch you," says Peter.
"Both," he adds.
This makes Dad laugh,
Makes me chuckle,

Makes Peter
Pound his chest.
"I'm the boss now," he says.

We stand
Above her,
Looking down,
The three of us.
Her men
That she lifted
Daily.
Forty-four years
For a lifetime is
Not enough.
She lies there.
Her men,
Her boys,
Worship her.
In only
Forty-four years,
She lived
More than most
Do in a
Lifetime.

I suddenly feel this need
To stand guard
Over her body.
My shoulders tall,
My head comes up.

I station myself
Near the front
Of the casket,
The brown wood
With flowers everywhere.
She's always
Protected me,
Now I am
Protecting her.
Her soul,
Her body,
Her absoluteness.

They filter in,
The hordes of people.
They file by a collage of photos
From Mom's youth.
From her twenties,
From her thirties.
Her forties
Barely entered.
Unfair.

Peter holds
Grandma's hand.
He's her favorite,
And why not?
I'm the freak,
The one who can't
Manage his emotions.

The one who cuts
Blood maps in his arms.
The one who went too far.
The one who took the rope,
Made a noose.
The one who lost it as he
Tightened it around his neck,
But never swung
To Death.

I'm damaged goods,
Torn apart
In my mind.
Mom held me
Together
Enough not to
Completely break
Or fall to
Pieces.
Will I now
Shatter
Like crystal
On ceramic tile?
No, I'm more like
A dirty window
From an old house
That's
Withering
With time.

Elementary school friends,
Middle school friends,
High school friends,
College friends,
Work friends,
Friends?

What does the word
"Friend" mean?
I only know two of
Mom's friends,
Kyle and Rose.
How can a
Hundred people be
"Friends"?
And I only know two?
Fuck friends!
Mom would have been proud
That I kept that in
My head.

They filter by,
Telling stories,
Laughing.
I want to
Explode.
I think they are all
Waiting for the
Potato salad.

The funeral home is empty
Except for the celebrant
Trying to look mournful,
His millionth death,
And Dad
And Peter
And Grandma,
Who clings to
Peter's arm
As if she will be
Blown away
If she lets go,
To become a
Part of the wind.
I wish I could
Become a
Part of the wind,
Drifting away from here.

One last time
To hold Mom's hand.
It's cool to the touch.
I want to climb in the casket
And lie next to her
Like when I was little,
Watching reruns of
The Andy Griffith Show.
Instead,
I kiss her head.

Caked-on makeup
Smears from my lips.
Mom hated makeup.
It doesn't even look like her,
Lying there,
Lifeless,
With painted cheeks.

She's gone.
I can feel that her
Soul has drifted
Somewhere,
Anywhere,
Nowhere,
Wherever souls go
When they no longer
Need their body.

Peter says,
"She's not there, Dylan."
He looks up.
"She's up there now."
He's right.
If anyone deserves Heaven,
It's Mom.
Peter says,
"She will be here when you need her."
"Like now," I whisper.
Peter hugs me.

The pallbearers,
Who I don't know,
Carry Mom to the hole
That was dug for her
By a machine
That sits in the distance,
Silently
Waiting
To cover her up.

Shouldn't I
Carry her?
Shouldn't Peter
Carry her?
Shouldn't Dad
Carry her?
Traditions
Suck!

A minister says a
Few words
About a woman he
Doesn't know
Except for the stories
Dad told him.
Not sure why Dad
Agreed to do this.
We don't go to church.
The minister sees my frown.
You don't fucking know her.

Mom would have been proud
That I kept that in my head.
"Grandma wanted it." Dad leans in.
He must have seen
My fidgeting
To fake words
From an insincere mouth.

The pallbearers
Stand tall.
I shiver as he
Catches my eye,
Uncle Kipp.
He gives me a
Sly grin.
Body stiffens,
Muscles tight,
Breathing increases.
I want to escape.
Here comes
Another
Fucking
Panic!

I turn to leave,
But Peter holds me.
His touch is welcome.
Uncle Kipp's wasn't
So long ago.

I turn.
TJ and three
Mourning people
behind me, crying.
He sees my need to
Escape.
TJ knows.
He's the only one
I ever told
About
Uncle Kipp.

TJ mouths,
"You okay?"
I'm not okay!
Mom is dead.
They want to
Throw
Dirt
All over her,
And Uncle Kipp
Threw
Dirt
All over me
With his
Filthy hands.
I'm not fucking okay!

Peter is rubbing my back.
The attack,
The War

In my head my
Panic continues.
People are looking now.
Vulnerable.
Dad leans in.
"You okay, buddy?"
I take a heavy step back,
Plead to Mom
Through a wooden box,
Mind screaming,
To come out and
Help me.
It's building,
It's boiling,
It's exploding.
"Get me the fuck out of here..."
My voice,
It surges.
"You're all a bunch of fucking phonies."
Mom would
Not
Have been proud
I didn't keep that in
My head.
It came out
Of a mouth
And head
That's spinning
Out of control.
I run.

FOUR

TJ's car,
The smell of air freshener
And body spray
And weed,
Trying too hard
To mask a smell
Of comfort.
Inhale,
Calm.

"Let's eat.
How about Bridges?" says TJ,
My only friend.
"Can't believe that
Fucking pervert was there."
His anger shows.
Disgust!
"He should be in jail."
TJ takes a hit and passes it.
Embarrassment!
"Then he would get payback.
I heard that they don't like pedophiles."
TJ stops directly in front of Bridges.
Humiliation!
"We should get that asshole back."
TJ grips his steering wheel tighter.

Shame!
"Let's eat." TJ snaps his fingers in
Front of my face. "You there?"
Revenge!

I chew on microwaved eggs,
All the coffee shop can muster,
Cheese grease on my hands.
I'm high,
Too high,
And I overly appreciate
The addiction of cheese.
"Fuck, this is good!"
I say, smiling at the cheese.
I sip a latte,
And then I vomit.

We exit Bridges.
Back in the car.
No mercy for the weak.
That's what I am,
Weak.

He took so much from me:
Innocence,
Youth,
Purity,
Cleanliness,
Light,

Strength,
Oxygen,
Hope.

And he gave me so much:
Anxiety,
Depression,
Panic,
Trauma,
Fear,
Loss,
Disgust,
Filth.

FIVE

Home.
Phone rings.
"You okay, buddy?"
Dad sounds tired.
"I'm good."
"I know this is tough on you."
I nod as if he can see me.
"TJ said he had you, so I left you alone."
Noise in the background.
Peter!
"Let me talk to him," says Peter.
I smile with the taste of vomit
As Peter's voice brings security.
"You breathe," he says.
"Do yoga.
You're missing the sandwiches."
The thought of sandwiches to
Celebrate a life
Almost makes me vomit again.
"I'll get something here," I say.
"Take care of Dad."
Peter is gone.
Dad says, "Get some rest.
I'll be home in a little while."
Rest?
"Oh, and I have a call out to your therapist.
You need to get in this week."

Crazy me,
On display.

Losing it.
I have lost
Something,
Everything!
Mom,
Dignity,
Strength,
Innocence.

I lay back
On my bed,
Looking at a poster
Of Bruce Springsteen.
Seems The Boss
Could write about this,
My life.

I cover my head
With the pillow,
Scream,
Cry.
Trying
To suffocate
The pain.

Memories
Like shards of glass

Cutting my mind,
Trying to find the pieces,
Glue the thoughts
Together
To form the story
That is my life.

SIX

The story:

I was twelve.
Mom and Dad and Peter
And me,
Family vacation,
Road trip.
Peter telling jokes
In the back seat
For a thousand miles.
Albuquerque, New Mexico.

The arrival:

Shallow hugs
From grandparents
I hardly know
And an uncle
I thought of as
Cool from stories
Mom told me.

One day:

Mom and Dad
Stayed back with Grandma.

Peter with Grandpa fishing.
Uncle Kipp took me hiking.
He seemed like the world
Was his.
Everything was his.
Strong,
Handsome,
Confident.

We hiked
Far enough
Where my
Twelve-year-
Old legs
Suffered
The rocky
Ascent.
Tired,
Hungry,
But I loved
The mountains,
The thin air,
The view,
And the
Feeling
It gave me,
Like I was on
Top of the world.

Isolated:

Looking over the
Rocky ledge,
Uncle Kipp's
Arm around
My shoulder,
Still okay,
Arm to
My back,
Still okay,
Arm to
My waist,
Uncomfortable!
Arm to
My leg,
Trying to move.
Pulled closer,
Forceful.
"Stop!"
My voice
Bellowed.
Pulled to the
Ground,
"Stop!"
Held down,
"Stop!
My hands
Can't move.
His do.

Shock.

Force.
Pain.
Screaming.
Muffled.
Hand over mouth.
Silence.

Shock.

"You better never tell anyone," he says.
Silence.
"...You wanted to anyway."
Silence.
"...You came here with me."
Silence.
"...You just need to forget about it."
Silence.
"...You say anything and you will look bad."
Silence.
"...You say anything and I'll hurt Peter."
Silence.
"...You are to blame anyway."
Silence.

SEVEN

Back to the present:

Pillow removed
From a wet face.
Dad knocks,
Walks in.
I'm half-asleep.
Panic drains you of
Everything.
Exhaustion.
Dad sits on
The edge
Of my bed.
I can tell
It's about to
Become a
Father-and-son moment,
Like many times before:
Girls,
How to fight,
Drugs,
Grades,
Sex,
Integrity,
Character,
Responsibility.

The talk I really need?
How to love myself.
Forgive myself.

"You doing okay?" asks Dad.
I wipe my eyes clear.
"This is going to take time," he says.
Both hands comb
Through my hair.
My fingers hurt.
"Mom was our rock."
Dad is struggling.
I rise up on my elbows.
"She's still with us,
Always." Dad can't accept
Her death either.
I nod in agreement.
At least I want to
Believe him.
I want to believe
Peter when he says,
"I can still talk to her."
Dad touches my arm,
And it's comforting as always.
"I'm here for you."

Secure.
Strong.
Dad would kill Uncle Kipp if he knew.

"We will get through this together.
Loss is a part of life, Dylan.
The hardest part, but
We need to learn from loss, and
Everything your mom
Has taught you still matters,
More than ever.
What she taught Peter matters.
What she taught me matters.
She matters."
I know he's right.
She does matter.
Dad matters,
Peter matters,
TJ matters,
Do I?

EIGHT

"That was a long time ago. Why now?"
Asks TJ as we sit in his car.
The school parking lot is
Full.
Full of the cliques
Rolling up in their Beamers and Lexus.
Full of shit.
Me, I mean.
That's how I feel for
Letting something bother me
That happened six years ago.
Full of shit.
I should bury it, but I can't.
"I haven't seen him in years,
Since I was thirteen," I reply.
"Remember that time he
Showed at our house
And I ran away,
Hiding in the woods, and
You came and found me?"
TJ nods. "That's when you told me."
"Mom and Dad thought I ran away because
They grounded me for skipping school."
Pause.
"I was afraid that fucker came to see us because
He wanted to rape me again."
"What now?" TJ looks at me.

"Dad says therapy.
He thinks it's because of Mom."
I play with the door.
"Maybe you should kill him," says TJ.
"I could help."
A thought enters.

What happened in school today?
All a blur.
Been gone for a week
After Mom's funeral.
Dad said, "It's time to return.
It'll be tough but good for you."
So what happened?
History: teaching it all wrong.
Physics: don't care and confusing.
Lunch: uncomfortable stares and leaned-in whispers.
Study Hall: more uncomfortable stares and leaned-in
    whispers.
Creative Writing: just what I needed. Ninety minutes
    of writing in a journal.
Peter: hallway hugs, high fives, resilience, the best
    human I know.

Back in TJ's car.
"You going to do it?" he asks.
He doesn't start the car.
I'm becoming anxious.
"That fuck deserves to die," he continues.
Uncle Kipp's face

Fills my mind.
"He's still around.
I asked your dad when I was
At your house yesterday."
Breathing is heavy.
"Sorry, dude,
Don't want to get you riled up."
TJ pauses.
Everything is getting blurry,
A familiar feeling.
I'm spinning.
"I just...I'll help you."
TJ pulls away.
Whose death
Do I want more?
Mine or Kipp's?

Driving home
In silence,
TJ takes the long way,
Hoping I'll calm.
I do when
I see Peter
Get off the bus,
Something he does
To gain independence.
Peter waves
Then runs inside.
Reruns of *Star Trek* await,
His routine.

I need one,
A routine.
Not sure killing
Uncle Kipp
Is it.

TJ, "You good?"
I nod.
We fist-bump.
"No worries," I say.
TJ, "I'm sort of kidding."
He sees the look in my eyes,
One he's seen since we were little.
Worries about the reality of his suggestion
Fill his eyes.
"I'm good," I assure him.

My mind is a fucking mess
That I want to sweep into the storm drain
Below my feet as I step out of the car.
That's what I want, to be swept away.

NINE

A month passes.
Grieving gets worse.
Therapy tomorrow.
It took a month.
This is what
Teens go through,
Waiting a month
To get professional
Help.
That's why weed
Is smoked,
Why pills
Are swallowed,
Why death
Is a reality.
Fucking shame.

My appointment interrupts
Creative writing class,
The class I need most
To get my thoughts down
And out
Of my head.
Thoughts that keep
Fucking with me
Big-time.

Thoughts telling me that
I should kill him.
An internal dialogue
Of murdering a man
That stole so much
From me.
I didn't do anything,
Say anything.
He left without consequence
And I
Betrayed myself,
Betrayed my youth,
Betrayed my innocence,
Betrayed!

Therapy:

"How are you doing..."
He pauses as he looks at his clipboard.
 "...Dylan?" he says, making sure he had the
Correct patient.
Fake smile, like he cares.
Who the fuck is this?
So I ask, "Who the fuck are you?"
Mom wouldn't have been proud.
"Dr. Little," he responds.
I almost laugh because he really is
A small man.
One of Peter's hugs would crush him.
"Where's Dr. John?" I ask.

Dr. Little shifts in his leather chair
That he has raised to be just
Above eye level from me,
His feet close to dangling.
"Your insurance doesn't cover
Meeting him anymore.
I thought you knew."
I feel warm, then hot,
And start to sweat,
And then cold and goosebumps
Slither across my arms.
Going from hot to cold so fast,
I wonder
If I will create a
Storm
And become
A tornado.
A hurricane?
"Nobody told me."
I want to leave,
Escape
From this man, Little.
Run from him.
I ran toward Dr. John
For three years.
He actually helped.
Gone.
Abandoned!

Dr. Little sets his clipboard down,
Yellow paper with scribble,
Some sort of writing,
His first assessment
Of my mind.

"Let's do an activity," he says.
I nod.
"Why not?"
He replies, "Okay."
He moves next to me
On the couch,
Too close.
I don't like men
Besides Dad, Peter, and TJ
Being close.
So close,
I can feel the warmth
Of his body.
It gives me chills
And a moment of nausea.

"I want to take you through a
Mindfulness activity," he says.
I chuckle.
"Are you familiar with mindfulness?"
"Very! My mom taught me, and so did
My yoga teacher."
"Then you should be a natural.
You are already very calming

To be around."
Creeped out.
I move closer to the
Edge of the couch,
Look at the door,
Look at the letter opener on his desk.
Escape or stab him?
Whatever works.

"Let's listen to this mindfulness app."
He turns the volume up on his phone.
Ocean waves,
A woman's voice
Coaching us to breathe.
App ends.
No movement from Little,
Head down,
Chin on chest.
I wait,
Looking at the door,
The clock on the wall.
I wait.
Should I leave?
I wait.
Maybe I'll sneak out, but
I have to wait,
Too curious to see how long
This will last.
I do know
We will not last.

I'm done with therapy.
Little wakes up
Just over seventeen minutes later.
"Oh, I'm embarrassed," he says.
I am motionless,
Mindful of his awkwardness,
Mindful of his lack of professionalism,
Mindful that I am about to walk out.
"You just relax me," Little says with a crooked smile.
I'm out the door,
Controlling my middle finger from rising.
Never will I see Little again.

TEN

Time passes.
You can't stop
A ticking clock.
All you can do
Is smash it
Against a wall.
But time will live
Until you don't.

Winter break,
Holiday break,
Never Christmas break.
Not allowed
With the need for
Political correctness.
I do break.
My mind is
Destroyed and
I feel like a stain
That covers the earth.
I need to be removed,
Cleansed.

I hate school.
It's a double-edged sword
Cutting deep.

I don't want to be there,
But when I'm not,
I suffocate,
I'm overwhelmed.
Thinking of the world,
My world,
Without structure,
The world seems
Too large,
Too busy,
Too dangerous,
Too much.

I would work.
It may help
But
Dad needs me with Peter
While he's at work.
Even though Peter
Needs me,
He is strong.
He's resilient.
He's addicting
To be around.
But Peter can't be
Alone.
I watch over
My big brother.
I watch his grace,
His ability to live,

And wish I had
His ability
To move through
The muck of life.

Christmas.
Two days
Until the birth
Of Jesus.
Is Mom with him?
Of course.
If she isn't,
Who could be?
I think about this
As presents barely fit
Under the stiff pine
In our living room.
Such a strange tradition
To place a tree
In a house
And try to keep it
Alive for three weeks.
I'm not sure I can make it
Three weeks.

Mom's death,
Grieving,
Has caused
Darkness
Like no other,

A perpetual state of
Loss.
That's me,
I'm a loser.
I'm losing everything:
My mind,
My happiness,
My hope,
My courage,
My ability
To continue.

And so it happens
One day,
Late afternoon.
Dad's at work,
Peter is watching *Star Trek*.
He will be there until Dad is home.
And so it happens
With a sudden sense
Of extreme clarity.
I smile as
I realize the pain
Will be over.
The pain of grieving
For my mom,
For a childhood
That I lost,
That was taken from me
On a mountain trail.

The pain
Will vanish with one
Drop,
One tight belt
Around my neck.
I clear a pile of clothes
From the closet floor.
I say goodbye
To Bruce,
Guitar and headband,
The Boss's hand raised
Hanging on my wall.
The Boss knows
Pain.
It's in his words,
Lyrics about life.

The noose is tied,
The leather is worn,
The pressure chokes
Just a little.
The belt is
Cool around
My neck.
Ready to go,
Ready to die,
To end life,
To not feel.
I start to cry.
Bruce looks down.

"Born to Run"
Screams in my head.
To live is what it's about,
But my hand strokes the belt.
I need to drop,
I need to feel
No more,
Nothing.

Peter turns the knob
To a locked door.
He knocks.
He bangs.
Should I drop?
He screams my name,
"DYLAN!"
He kicks.
Should I drop?
The door crashes open.
Splintered wood falls
To a carpeted floor.
Should I drop?

Peter charges me.
I'm on the floor
Next to a pile of clothes.
He's on top of me
Pulling the belt from my neck.
I take a full breath.
It makes me dizzy.

Peter crushes my chest
By sitting on me,
Squeezing me.
He's always been strong.

"Dylan, you don't do that."
Shame.
"Dylan, you need to smile more."
Guilt.
"Dylan, you need to talk to Mom."
Selfish.
"Dylan, you tell her you love her."
Truth.
"Dylan, I will help."
I gasp for breath.
"Say it!"
"Mom, I love you!"
I cry.

Peter pulls me up and
Out of the closet.
I can still feel the
Belt around my neck
Even though it's on the floor
Staring up at me.
It was my instrument to
Produce my own death, but
Peter gave me life.
He has always been
Stronger than me.

"We're going to talk to Mom," says Peter.
"I...I can't, buddy." I hold my head as I sit on my bed.
"Now!" demands Peter.
"I'm not sure what to say."
"Tell her you love her again.
You can't go wrong with love," Peter whispers
Close to my ear.
"Remember what the Beatles say,
'All you need is love.'"

Peter holds me with one arm around my shoulder.
He rubs my back, and then I start
To talk to a dead mother
That left me
Ruined.

"Mom," I say with hesitation.
I pause, waiting for
A sign,
A reply.
Peter is silent.
"Mom, I miss you."
I gulp for a breath.
"I need you."
My eyes are turning blurry.
"I'm going through a lot."
Tears are forming.
"And I can't do it by myself."
I place my head in my hands.
"I'm lost," I whisper.

"I'm not sure I can hold on."
Peter tightens his grip as if to tell me
He's got me.
"Secrets," I gasp.
"I've got secrets I need to tell."
Peter leans in to listen.
"When you left, and died,
I died a little more."
My jeans are soaked from
Falling tears.
"I'm angry." I grip my kneecaps.
"I'm so angry."
Guilt.
"That I couldn't save you."
Selfish.
"That you left me when I needed you most."
Grief.
"I just...miss you so much.
I miss our talks."

Peter with both hands on my shoulders.
"That's why you talk to her now," he says.
He turns my shoulders to make me face him.
"You never stop talking to her."
Peter bear-hugs me,
Pulls me up onto my feet.
"I love you, Dylan."
I gasp for enough air to say,
"I love you too."
Peter is strong.

ELEVEN

Dad by the tree
Christmas morning,
Head in hands,
The pile of presents before him,
Attempt at normalcy.
Red paper
With snowmen
And Santa
To mask the pain.
I slide onto the couch
Next to him.
Warmth.
He hugs me.
Peter is next to us.
He pries his body
Between us,
Hugging us both.
"I told Mom I would
Take care of you,"
Peter whispers.
"It'll be okay."
Dad cries,
I cry,
Peter says a little louder,
"Right, Mom?"
Laughter mixed with tears.
I knew the holiday would be

Smashing our emotions
Like a broken ornament
Fallen from the tree,
But Peter brings strength
Unknown to most.

TJ shows,
Gift in hand,
Tradition
Since we were
Eight.
He comes
Bearing gifts
For me,
For Peter,
For Dad,
For Mom.
He has them all.

The difference,
This time
His dad, Brad,
His mom, Olivia,
Come with him.
Their hugs feel
Comforting,
Especially from his
Mom.
We need a
Woman

In our house.
We need a
Woman's
Strength,
Comfort,
Laughter,
Care.

They pray,
Olivia,
Brad,
TJ.
Dad pretends
By bowing his head.
I give intentions,
Something I do
In yoga
And Mom taught me
Over a decade ago.
Peter pretends to
Pray by saying,
"To boldly go
Where no man has
Gone before, Amen."
Laughter,
Much needed,
Followed by tears
And more laughter.
The best drain of energy
While feeling pain

Is laughter.
Release.

Wrapping paper everywhere.
Chain stores are doing well
With selling t-shirts, socks, and underwear.
Mom obviously did the Christmas shopping
In past years.
One present remains,
It awaits under the tree.
Dad nudges me.
"That's for you," he says.
My hands seem to have lost their ability to
Move
And so have my legs.
Too much turkey,
Or too much
Grief.
Peter hands it to me.
I slowly tear the edges and then
Rip it open.
Before me is Mom and me.
I'm twelve,
Smiling while leaning into her
On a mountaintop in New Mexico.
I remember the drive
To the lookout and how we hiked
The mile to the edge.
A steep drop below,
Mom screamed with delight,

"I love this,"
To the thin air.
Then grabbed me and
Squeezed me
Into her side.
I squeezed back,
And just as our cheeks combined,
Dad shot the picture.
It's here in front of me,
Evidence I was once happy,
The day before I
Hiked with Uncle Kipp.

I freeze
And then fight for breath,
Escape
To my bedroom.
TJ follows.
No scene,
Just two teenage boys
Heading off on their own.
TJ knows the signs and
Made our exit normal.
On my bed
Holding my head,
Rapid heart.
TJ sits on the floor.
"Hard to see your mom?" he says.
"Hard to see me happy," I reply.
"What?"

"It was the day before."
"Fuck."
"Fuck" sums it up well.

"I still think
We should kill him," says TJ.
He looks serious,
Scares me on
Christmas Day.
Then he looks at
Bruce on my wall
With talk of murder
Lingering.
"Road trip. We could
Drive down there and take him."
He still looks at Bruce.
Bandana, guitar, cut-off sleeves.
"Born to run, right?" says TJ.
I calm, distracted
By murder,
By revenge.
"And then what?" I ask.
TJ adjusts to face me.
"Then you live a happy life
Knowing that fucker is gone."
The problem?
Once something has been done,
It can't be undone.
"Think about it. I'll drive."
Pause.

"Your piece of shit car
Wouldn't make it down there."
Laughter.
Much needed to
Break the thoughts
Of killing.
Christmas is over.

TWELVE

Semester starts,
New class,
New teacher.
He opens class
By singing a song.
Laughter erupts.
This guy just ruined
Himself
Singing to teens.
He shows passion,
Laughter stops.
We lean in.
Different.
He sings
"No Hard Feelings"
By the Avett Brothers.
I know them.
Connection.

Hesitant
At first.
My last semester
As a high schooler
And the new guy
Wants us to listen to songs.
Really listen and
"Absorb words,"

He says,
"Swallow emotions,"
He says,
"Feel life,"
He says.
I'm hooked.
I need to feel
Something.
Anything!

Bell rings.
Lingering back,
Pretending
To search
The bottom of my
Backpack,
Rummaging around.
He approaches casually.
"Avett Brothers fan?"
I nod.
"I could tell when you
Mouthed a couple lyrics."
Guard down,
Vulnerable.
"You ever tried writing a song?"
No words emerge from
My throat.
Dry mouth,
Nervous.

Teachers never talk to me.
Why this guy?

Zipped bag,
Slow shuffle,
Still can't talk.
"Do you like to write?" he asks.
Already forgetting
His name,
I nod,
Finding words
Somewhere deep.
"I'm no good," I say.
"Nonsense," is his reply.
"I will prove it," I think
To myself.
"Head Full of Doubt,"
Another Avett Brothers song,
I think as
My head doubts me.
"Minds are meant to create."
He sees my
Lack of confidence.
It must scream out.
"Well, I need to go," I say.
"Yeah, bells do keep ringing." He smiles.
"See you, Mr..."
"Johnson." He smiles.
Judgment?

"Remembering a name is tough." Still smiling.
No judgment.
Mr. Johnson steps in the hall,
Waving at kids
That wave back.

Connections are made
By opening the portals
To our hearts and minds,
Allowing others in,
Except
I can only do so in hesitance
To protect myself.

THIRTEEN

Yoga mat folded,
Will she notice?
It's been four months
Since I've been in the
Heated room.
Maybe she won't from
Child's Pose,
Forehead on my mat.
Our bodies start to
Breathe
In unison.
The heat,
Sweat,
Flowing.
Mind relaxed,
Something I miss.
On my back,
Breathing slowly,
The hardest pose,
Savasana.
In my head,
My intention still there,
Mom.
Always Mom.

She comes to my mat,
Sits cross-legged

On the wood floor.
Prudence,
Named after a
Beatles song.
Hippie parents?
Or maybe just good taste.
"I'm so glad you made it," says Prudence
Softly.
"So am I." Smiling.
Yogis leaving with
Rolled-up mats.
"Have you been practicing?" she asks.
"No." Head falls.
"Don't do that." She smiles,
Gentle.
"Yoga will find you when you are ready," says
Prudence.
"I still breathe," I say.
"Then you are practicing."
Mom would be proud.
"Are you grieving?"
????????????
Hesitant.
"Have you let yourself grieve?" she restates.
"I'm drowning," I say.
I do grieve for the
Loss of
Mom
And me.

Guilt.
"Then you need to swim," says Prudence.

The room is cooling,
Lights low.
Prudence sits relaxed
But strong,
Like a boulder
In the middle of a wildflower field,
Like Mom,
Unmovable
But graceful.
I wish
I could be
Graceful in
Mind
And
Body.

"Dylan, it's okay to feel."
Tears.
"It's okay to show emotion."
Crying.
Prudence hugs
Like Mom,
Gentle but secure.
I melt
Into her gray hair
That falls over her shoulders.

"I miss her," I say.
Her hands on my shoulders.
"And that's okay," she says.
"I feel guilty." I look at Prudence.
"And that's okay too."
Prudence sees my breath increase.
"Let's breathe."
We breathe in and out,
Slowly,
Deeply.
In through my nose,
Out through my nose.
Calming.
"Feelings are normal.
Emotion is normal.
Never fight your feelings
Or you are fighting yourself,
And that's a battle
You never win."
Dear Prudence,
My yoga mom.

FOURTEEN

Mr. Johnson
Greets us by reading
A poem,
"Tulips"
By Sylvia Plath.
She seems to know,
Ms. Plath,
How I feel:
Darkness,
Hopeless,
Inanimate,
Nobody,
Broken,
Damaged goods.
I sigh,
Feeling understood.
Thank you,
Sylvia!
On a first-name basis
Now that we're friends
With similar darknesses.

"A poem..." says Mr. Johnson.
He leans in from the stool
He's perched on.
"...can tell you the truth..."
He raises his right hand to his temple.

"...can scare the hell out of you..."
He grasps Sylvia's book.
"...can offer you existence.
Do you believe that?"
Mr. Johnson pauses.
I shift in my seat,
Wanting to scream, "Yes!"
But this is high school,
Insecure adolescents
Trying to create an image.
Silence.
Giggling.
Whispers.
"Ah, then I wonder,
Why this class?"
We all look around at each other.
"If you don't believe words can
Create emotion,
Sending you to a
Different place and escaping
Your little worlds that you have created...
Then I wonder why you are here?"
With that,
More silence.

"You have the remainder of
Your time
To create emotion."
Mr. Johnson pauses
With a slight grin.

"Now go write."
We're released
Into thought.

I start to drift
Into the white paper
Before me
And write:
Before
I was human
Now I'm not
Flawed like a tree
Broken by the wind
Anguished by loss
An innocence
I barely remember
Something stolen
That will never return
Mercy
I beg
In order to leave my mind
My past
Behind
Or at least for my pain
To forgive me.

Mr. Johnson ends the class
With Robert Frost's poem
"The Road Not Taken."
Then he says,

"Leave now and take the road
Less traveled."
Laughter,
Smirks,
Confusion,
And headshakes.
And me,
Lingering back again.
"Dylan, I see you used
Your time
Wisely."
Wise is something I'm not.
I'm more like the invisible boy
Suffocating on his thoughts.
"I like being able to write," I say.
"Being able to write is like being able to run,"
Says Mr. Johnson.
He sees my puzzled look, then adds,
"It's freedom to escape."
"I guess," I say and head for the door.
He hands me a book,
A collection of poems
By Sylvia Plath.
"I think you will like it."
I nod, glancing at Ms. Plath's face
Looking
Melancholy.
Dark.
Hopeless.
In need of something,

Anything to fill her mind
Besides sadness.
"Thank you," I say
And add, "You're different
Than my creative writing
Teacher from last semester."
"Different can be good,"
Is Mr. Johnson's reply.
"It keeps us from settling,
Gathering dust."
The book travels with me
Through crowded hallways.
A sea of teenagers
Longing to feel normal.

FIFTEEN

It's just something I do,
Staring at the moon,
Trying not to cry.
Searching the shape
Of that big white ball
And the light that surrounds it.
Stars.
Contemplating my death,
Searching for hope to hang on to.
Any reason to live
While lying on the roof
Of a house in mourning.
A dad that is trying,
A brother that is able
To lend his strength to us all.
This roof has become
My sanctuary.

Can I find reasons
Not to die?
Can I find reasons
Not to live?
Can I find reasons
To keep going?
Can I find reasons
Not to take revenge?

On Uncle Kipp,
Or myself?

Cool breezes
With the smell of
Spring are distant.
It's coming,
Another season
Without Mom,
Another season
Without courage,
Another season
Without strength.

The feel of black shingles
Cools my back.
I pull weed from my pocket and
Smoke away the fears.
Mom wouldn't be proud.
I flick it off the side of the house,
A flame lit by movement and air.
It falls
What seems like a thousand-foot drop.
Extinguished.
That's me.
I cease to shine.

SIXTEEN

TJ plops down.
Literally, it's a
PLOP!
He does nothing silent.
Opens his lunch,
Shuffles his food,
Smacks his mouth.
Nothing is subtle
About my friend,
My only friend
Who is still obsessed
With killing
Uncle Kipp
And has me thinking,
Could we do it?

"Dude," says TJ.
"She's got her eye on you."
I look up from
Peanut butter and banana on wheat.
Extra peanut butter because Peter said
I needed protein,
And he spread it thick.
"Who?" I say. Words muffled,
Trying to hold food in my mouth.
"The new girl," says TJ.
"Haven't you heard about her?"

I shake my head "no" while the
New girl stares at me.
Transfixed by her beauty,
I start to sweat a little.
Auburn hair,
Beautiful without trying,
Natural.
I look back at my sandwich.
"She came from West High," says TJ.
West, the poor school.
The rich school is Roosevelt,
And we round out the city,
The middle class,
The balance.
"Truman High School,
The center of the universe,"
As one of our history teachers,
Mr. Brooks, likes to say as he rubs his crew cut.
"Be proud that we're named after a
Man who bombed the hell out of Japan and Korea."
I stay away from Mr. Brooks.
"Her dad must have gotten a better job," says TJ.
"Shut the fuck up," I reply,
"Not cool."
TJ sinks his face into his potato chip bag,
Emptying every last crumb.
"Yeah, you're right. Dumbfuck thing to say."
TJ sometimes speaks
Impulsively,
And it comes off as him being an asshole.

One thing that Mom taught me,
Amongst all the other things,
Was to speak up when people say
Degrading, rude things.
She would be proud.
"Anyhow, you want to
Hear about her or not?" asks TJ.
"Go," I say.

TJ goes on to tell me
About this auburn beauty
Who was raped at a high school party
When she was drunk
By the boy's cousin, who held the party,
And then the kid left to go back home
To Rockford, Illinois.
They arrested the boy.
He denied it.
His cousin backed him.
Off scot-free.
Her entire school started to bully her,
Like it was her fault because she was drunk,
Like it was her fault that she wore a skirt,
Like it was her fault that she flirted back.
No one did anything to help.
Tortured twice:
Rape,
Persecution.
We all heard,
All the way over here

At good ol' Truman High.
We heard about
The girl that was raped,
Like it was a flaw
Of hers.
As if she deserved it.
Her father found her
After taking a bottle
Full of pills.
A call to
911 and a
Pumped stomach
Saved her body.
But her mind,
I can imagine,
I know,
Is still fucked up.
She's with us,
New start,
New school,
New rumors.
How much can one person
Endure?

Her name is Audrey,
I find out through TJ,
Who seems to have the in on
Everything.
My interest is not in her beauty,
My interest is in her story.

To be violated,
Taken
Forcefully,
And for her rapist to be free,
Walking around
With no consequences,
Perhaps we should kill him too?

I don't know where
My thoughts will lead.
The anger and the
Desperation for justice are
Tearing me apart.
My mind seems to be
Fracturing
More and more.
I can't stop thinking about
Uncle Kipp's death
By my hands.
The asshole rapists that
Harmed Audrey and
Their deaths
By my hands.
My death
By my hands.
It's all whirling in my brain,
So much destruction,
So much violence.
I'm darkening,
Drowning,

Can't breathe.
It's what anger does,
Steals your identity
Until you become
Unrecognizable
To yourself.

I am skipping class again.
I have to be truant by now, and
I'm surprised
I haven't had a visit by the
Assistant principal,
Mr. . . . I don't know his name
Even though I've seen him a
Hundred times it seems.
That's usually his shitty job, or
The shoe-shined dean's,
To track down kids that
Don't want to be at school
And then try to convince them
Why they should.
Maybe it would be better to
Teach the teachers
How to engage us
With more than lessons on a
Screen or board or
Outdated books
And bring to us something real,
A connection,
That shows they care.

I haven't skipped
Mr. Johnson's class once because
I know he cares.
Through words and actions,
I know he cares.
Sometimes that's enough.

Mr. Johnson starts class
With a quote by Paulo Coelho:
"You drown not by falling into a river,
But by staying submerged in it."
I almost drop my pencil.
Holy shit!
I'm submerged in an ocean of
Guilt,
Pain,
Embarrassment,
Grief.
How can I swim out?

Mr. Johnson reads us some
More words from a book
Where he doesn't disclose the
Author's name,
But the words are powerful:
"You will become what you
Deserve,
By your actions,
Your dreams,
And how you live your life.

So go now,
And make yourself
Wonderful.
Create a self that you will be
Proud of, and live a life
Full of exhaustive laughter,
With a generous hand that will help others.
One that will bring fulfillment
On your own terms
Because it is your life after all.
Go live it with all your might."
And that is why I don't skip
Mr. Johnson's class.
He gives me something,
Everything, these days,
To look forward to.
And after his short reading,
He introduces her.
"Everyone, I want you to welcome
Audrey
To our writing space.
Just from my short talk with her,
I can tell she will offer a lot to our community."
She's here,
Two seats behind me and one over.
I can feel her looking.
"Now go write.
Take this uninterrupted space and create."

I open my journal and look at my last poem.
I realize how dark the words are, but it's
My truth.
I'm distracted by her presence.
I don't have much experience
With girls,
With talking or even being close to them.
I wish I did, but getting close to someone seems...
Dangerous.

Audrey suddenly appears
Next to me in the hallway.
I'm unsure if I should say,
"Hello,"
Or just leave my greeting
Within,
Someplace deep
Where everything else lies
Dormant by fear. I fear
That she may be afraid
Of boys
Like I became afraid
Of men.
I swallow my words and look down
At shoes that are worn.

Sweaty hands,
Anticipation.
"Hi, my name is Audrey," she says.

"I'm..."
Lost in thought,
Nervous,
Intimidated.
"...Dylan." My name is muffled.
She smiles and says,
"I thought maybe you forgot for a moment."
We both grin.
"I'm new." She nervously laughs.
"But I guess you know that from last class?"
I nod.
"Mr. Johnson is cool.
He seems to understand," she adds.
"Yeah, he's cool. It's the only class I like," I say.
I don't need to ask what she means by
"Understand"
Because it's simply life
That Mr. Johnson seems to
Understand.
"I hope you don't mind me being blunt?"
She brings me a moment of fear.
I'm trying to figure out if that's a question
I should answer.
"Go ahead," I say, anticipating what will come next.
"I heard some kids talking in class about
Your mom dying."
Frozen.
"I don't mean to upset you," she says.
"I just...I hate it when kids are gossips."

I look down and nod.
"So, I thought I would just say hello and tell you that
I don't think it's cool
For those assholes to bring up your mom, like it's a
Fucking Netflix special or something."
"I appreciate that," I say nervously.
"Okay, well, maybe we can have lunch
Tomorrow or something," she says.
"Yeah, that's cool," I say,
Trying to be cool.
Never works for me.
She smiles. "Will your friend care?"
"TJ? No, he won't care.
He's a goof sometimes, but he's good people."
Still not cool.
"Okay, I'll find you tomorrow." She waves
Goodbye and then turns.
"Stay gold, Ponyboy." Then she walks away.
I get the *Outsiders* reference, and suddenly
Audrey becomes one of the
Most interesting people I've met,
And in such a short moment,
So it must be
Real.

SEVENTEEN

The drive home,
Snow drifting,
Mind drifting,
Emotions drifting,
All blinding me.

"She already wants to have lunch?" asks TJ.
"I think she's lonely," I say.
"But...no offense, why you, dude?"
"Because I'm ridiculously handsome?"
We laugh
At the truth that I'm average,
Whatever the fuck that word means.
Self-judgment
On a lanky body.
Self-judgment
On a thin face.
Self-judgment
On uncombed hair.
Body-shaming.
Mom always said,
"Say something nice about yourself."
And I would search my mind,
Struggling to find even
One thing.
"I guess I like my eyes"
Was always my reply.

A deep blue surrounded
By red and white.
The red being the only part
I don't like, but the red
Shows truth.

"You know." TJ paused.
"You're not a bad-looking guy,
You just need to work out or something.
Build up those arms and chest a little."
My reply, "Fuck you."
And we laugh.
Grateful
To laugh.
And that's friendship,
To laugh when there is
So much to cry about.

EIGHTEEN

Dad,
Dressed in workout clothes,
Home already,
Peter next to him.
Star Trek isn't
Screaming from Peter's room.
Unusual.
"Hey, buddy," Dad says.
"We thought we would go to
Yoga with you."
I pause. "I wasn't going tonight."
Confused.
"Well, I thought it would be
Good for us all, and Peter is excited."
Dad is trying.
He wants to help me,
Help Peter,
Carry our weight,
Our grief.
I see it on his face.
It's become dark,
Darker,
And thinning.
Perhaps yoga will help him,
So I agree.

Prudence greets us.
"Dylan, my lovely,
Who do you have with you today?"
Peter gives a simple "What's up?" like he's seen her
A hundred times.
"This is my dad, Tom, and my brother, Peter."
I gesture with my head.
Dad reaches his hand out and
Shakes Prudence's hand.
She's older than him, but
I can see from his stare
Immediate attraction.
Not just to her beauty, with her gray hair
That seems to
Bring out her eyes,
But her calmness.
It's immediate and addicting.
"It's good to meet you," says Dad.
Suddenly, I look at my dad for the first time
As a single man,
And it makes my heart race
Knowing he could marry again one day,
Giving me a new mom.
Fuck no!
My thoughts spin.
Prudence hugs me and
Stops the spinning.
Calmness.
"Thank you for coming."
She grips my hands in hers.

"Dylan can show you what to do.
Just take it slow,"
She says to Peter and Dad.
"Cool," says Peter and takes the lead
Into the studio.

On our mats,
Heated air,
Giving an intention.
Needed.
Mine goes to
Audrey,
Which surprises me.
It's always given to Mom.
Something tells me
Audrey needs it.
If her pain
Is like mine,
I know she needs it.
Dad keeps his eyes closed.
Peter is watching me,
Smiles when he sees me look at him.
I wink.

We flow,
Dad stumbling,
Peter so flexible.
He makes it look easy,
Like he's been practicing for years,
Which he has,

Except at home
Or in a grassy field
With Mom.
Never at the studio
Because of *Star Trek*
And potato chips.
Why now?
How?
I hate it when my mind
Drifts during yoga:
Focus,
Mindful,
Namaste,
Complete.

I wait as always.
Routine.
Prudence sits next to me.
Dad seems confused,
Peter is still on his back,
Eyes shut.
Savasana seems natural, easy.
I envy him.
"I'm so glad you came," says Prudence,
Looking at Dad,
Who sits back down
On his mat.
"Thanks," he says,
"I know Dylan needs it.
We all do."

Prudence smiles.
It's warming and gentle.
There are some people
In this world
Who are healers.
After a check-in
With how we feel,
Prudence says,
"Anything new in your life, Dylan?"
I'm quiet.
I know Dad wanted to fill a gap
For Mom by coming here,
But suddenly I'm cautious.
Dad kneels, rolls his mat.
"Peter, let's go to the car."
He wipes sweat from his forehead.
"One second," says Peter.
He is surprisingly
Awake.
"We need to go," Dad says to Peter.
"I need to tell Mom goodbye."
Peter is more awake than all of us
For many reasons.
They leave the room.
"Take your time," says Dad.
"Very nice to meet you."
Prudence brings her hands together.
"Namaste!" she says.

"I met someone interesting," I share.
"Tell me," says Prudence.
"A girl." We both smile.
"Who has pain."
Prudence stops smiling.
Empathy.
"Pain like mine." I stop.
"She lost someone?" asks Prudence.
"No...not really someone."
I have been having conversations like this
With Prudence since I was twelve.
Twelve,
That age where I was unsure why I felt this way,
Compartmentalizing pain,
Rape.
"Herself," I say.
I stop myself because not even Prudence
Knows
Everything
About my darkness.

Pain resonates
Within my mind,
Shoulders,
And hands.
My hands tingle,
A flushing of anxious blood fills them.
The flushing goes to my arms
And feet and face
And eyes.

The eyes are the worst.
They cause blurred vision,
And I already struggle to see the world.

Prudence can tell I'm holding something in
Deep, where the bad things live.
She never pushes too hard,
Just enough
To leave me with something to think about.
"Dylan, sometimes people with so much pain
Find each other. They do so in a way that either heals
    them and
Puts their broken pieces back together, or splinters
    their hearts
To an unrepairable mess."
I look up when she says "unrepairable mess."
Is that what I am?
Then I picture Audrey.
"I think, maybe, we can heal each other," I say.
Prudence smiles.
I continue, "I can't explain it.
I don't even know if it's real.
I just met her, and maybe it seems crazy,
but there's something about her
That brings out something about me
To want to talk to her
And maybe help her just by being there."
Prudence, with a slight gesture,
Welcomes me to lean in,
And in a soft voice,

The type of voice that makes
You listen a little harder,
She says, "I think maybe Audrey has shown up
During this time in your life for a reason,
So explore each other and find out why."

Prudence has pain.
Prudence has a past.
Prudence was abused.
Prudence was married.
Prudence was trapped.
Prudence escaped.
Prudence found her life.
Prudence regained strength.
Prudence always had it.
Prudence was tested.
Prudence overcame.
Prudence is real.
Prudence is resilient.

We hug.
Prudence smiles.
"Dylan, I'm not sure what this is."
She has tears.
"Don't question it." She looks into my eyes.
I stare back with love, a similar stare I gave to Mom.
"Just let it flow," she says.
She has always been there for me,
Along with Mom,
A woman who I look to as

Strong,
Resilient,
Peaceful,
Confident,
In pain.
"If this girl has come into your life
For a reason,
Don't fight it.
Let it happen naturally.
Give it time,
Space, and
Open your heart up to her."
I smile nervously and then frown.
"I feel crazy telling you
This because I just met her.
She made me feel...
In just a moment...like I have never felt."
"Never judge your feelings," says Prudence as she takes
My hands into hers.
"There are people that spend a lifetime together
That never make each other feel like you did
In one single moment."

Dad drives.
Silence.
Until,
"Prudence is interesting," he says.
Describing her like I did Audrey to Prudence,
Not sure how that makes me feel.
I nod as if he can hear my head move.

"Mom mentioned her often.
I just never got it," says Dad.
"She's..."
"Serene," I add.
"Tranquil," Dad finishes.
And as we both slightly smile,
Slowly breathe,
Relaxed in our agreement,
Peter adds, "Mom says hello."
Peter is a healer too.

NINETEEN

I can't explain it.
I'm not sure I want to.
I still feel pain
From losing Mom,
And the pain
From Uncle Kipp,
But I found something
To look forward to.
The excitement
Of seeing her grows
Deep within.
What is this new feeling?
Hope?

TJ rushes to class,
Physics test awaits.
He thinks he wants to be a doctor
Or a chiropractor,
So he loaded up on science
His senior year.
I'm lingering outside
The high school,
Waiting for the bell to ring,
Not sure about first hour.
I convince myself I'll wait
Until Mr. Johnson's class,
And then he's there,

Next to me,
Mr. Johnson.

"Hey there." He reaches out and
Knuckles. A fist bump later,
We are talking.
"Spring is coming," Mr. Johnson says.
I nod in agreement.
"Dylan, how are you doing?"
He's opening a door.
Do I go through it,
Let him enter my thoughts?

"I'm okay," I reply.
Unsure.
"Are you?"
He pauses after his question.
"Some days," I say.
"That's better than no days,
I suppose," he says.
I nod and grin.
The final bell rings.
Neither of us move.
Mr. Johnson suggests a bench.
We sit.
He doesn't seem like the type
To lecture,
But I wait,
Anticipating a talk
About why I'm not in class.

"How are you feeling about
Your mom?" he asks.
I shrug.
He continues, "Are you allowing
Yourself to grieve?"
"I'm not sure." I struggle to
Allow myself anything,
Let alone grief.
"What are you feeling?"
I say nothing,
Maybe because
Nothing is how I feel,
Especially this morning
Because that's how I woke up,
Feeling numb,
Nothing.
"You don't have to talk about it,"
Mr. Johnson says,
Then leans forward with elbows on knees.
"I lost a friend a while back." He looks at the cement
Below his boots, brown, worn leather meeting concrete.
"He was a veteran, home from Iraq for a short leave.
We served together for six years, but when the war started,
He went and I became a teacher."
Mr. Johnson leans back and
Searches the sky.
I know that look
Of searching the sky
For answers to questions
That remain untold.

"My friend became depressed.
He saw unimaginable things,
Things that no one should have to see.
Then, before his next deployment,
He killed himself."
I look quickly at Mr. Johnson,
Not shocked,
Simply interested and trying to show
Empathy.
"I felt so much guilt." Mr. Johnson
Stops searching the sky
And nods at a student passing.
He continues, "My guilt was for many reasons:
Not saving him,
Not being there enough,
Leaving the service when
I should have been with him,
Becoming a teacher while he was fighting,
And well...everything.
I was consumed by
Guilt,
Anger,
Fear, and
Sadness."
I've never had a
Conversation like this with a teacher.
I never talk to men like this,
Only Mom and Prudence,
But never men, not even Dad.
It is...real...refreshing...validating.

"I finally realized that
I couldn't have stopped him.
See, death is out of our control,
Especially when someone wants to
Produce their own.
However, that doesn't take away the
Guilt,
Pain,
Or any other
Feeling."
"When did this happen?" I ask.
"Ten years ago."
Mr. Johnson shakes his head in disbelief.
"Ten years went by like a heartbeat. Fuck!"
He pauses. "Sorry."
I shrug off his swearing and he continues.
"I still have his number in my phone.
His name is there, and sometimes I just look at it or
Even dial it to see if it was real.
If he is dead,
And will he answer?"
I know how that is and nod, then say,
"I thought I was the only one who did that."
Mr. Johnson looks over at me and waits.
I go on, "I look at my mom's number every morning
And then call it to tell her I'm going to school.
I look at it every night
And call it to leave her a voicemail to
Tell her goodbye.
I'm afraid..." I stop myself.

"Of what?" Mr. Johnson asks.
"That one day I'll hear that her voicemail is full
And I can't leave a message."
"Talking to the dead is a gift." Mr. Johnson smiles.
"I talk to my buddy every day
On the way to school.
He's why I'm here."
"What do you mean?" I say.
"Just before he died, he told me to become a teacher."
Mr. Johnson shakes his head and smiles.
"Well, he wasn't quite that gentle.
He actually said,
'Quit wasting your fucking life.
You should become a teacher.
Kids need you.
You'd be good at it.'"
Then Mr. Johnson laughs.
I know that laugh.
It isn't a laugh that he's
Sharing at this moment with me.
It's one he shares with his friend.
I know because TJ and I share that same laugh,
One that only the bond of friendship knows.
"I tell you." He pauses.
"I became a teacher, and I'm not sure if I'm any good at it
Or the one he wanted me to be, but I try."
"How have you moved on?" I hesitantly ask.
I'm afraid of the answer.
"I haven't," says Mr. Johnson.
"I'm not sure we ever

'Move on' from death.
I believe we are in a perpetual state of grieving.
It's part of life. It's how we pick up the
Fallen, broken pieces that matter."

We continue to talk about
Our broken pieces,
Friendship,
Family,
Depression,
Grief,
Anxiety,
Guilt,
Healing,
Coping,
Resilience.
And then the bell rings for second period.
We walk to my class.

Mr. Johnson pats my shoulder.
My trust grows for another man,
Something I didn't know I was
Capable of, but wanted.
Needed.

TWENTY

The smell of hot dogs,
That rubbery meat on a bun,
Fills the cafeteria air.
I've never anticipated lunch
This much before.
Will she show?
Will she remember?
Was she serious?
I actually cleaned my shoes,
Washed my jeans,
Wore my best hoodie.
Second impressions.

TJ plops down.
As always, he makes
His presence
Known.
I don't know if
I want him here
To be my wingman for this
Inauguration of
Female conversation.

"What's going on?" asks TJ.
"What do you mean?"
"Something's different," he says.
"About what?"

"You!
You seem different."
He looks at me closely,
Examining me.
"Did you try to comb your hair?"
The accusation of hair-combing
Lingers for a moment.
"Yeah, that's it," he says
And continues with his interrogation.
"Why? I told you years ago to just leave
That wavy mess alone." He laughs.
I smile, then a gentle, "Fuck you."
"That had to cause some morning pain...
Trying to run a comb through that."
"Brush," I say.
"That brush lost," says TJ.

She appears,
Sits across from me,
Next to TJ,
Not looking at him
But me.
I sit straight,
Palms sweating.
TJ is silent,
First bite of sandwich
Sitting in his mouth,
No experience with girls either.
Both of us frozen,
Teenage testosterone statues.

"What's up?" Audrey says
Like she's talked to me forever.
"Not much," I try to say with some
Confidence and coolness.
TJ is still frozen with ham and cheese
Clearly in his mouth.
Audrey takes fruit from her cloth bag.
"Are you going to introduce me to the guy staring at me
With half-chewed lunch meat?" She giggles.
I laugh. TJ swallows whatever's in his mouth whole.
"This is TJ," I say.
Audrey lays her hand out for TJ to shake,
And he does with hesitance.
Probably the first teenage girl
That he's touched, and inexperience shows.
"Is it still cool that I eat here?" Audrey asks.
"Of course," I say.
Prudence told me to be myself.
I relax within myself and breathe slowly,
Trying to be calm, which strangely
Is not myself.

"How long have you known each other?" Audrey asks.
"Since we learned to tie our shoes," I say.
Laughter.
TJ gets comfortable within himself too.
"Yeah, but I learned first and then had to help this guy
Because the other kids were making fun of him at recess."
TJ reaches his fist out for a bump.
I give him knuckles.

"Batman and Robin, right?" says TJ.
I nod and laugh,
Growing comfortable in my skin
And hair, knowing it has crawled back
To its original position by now.
"Does that make me Catwoman?" Audrey says.
Do we have a third?
Another to join us?
In this world of unknowns,
Damaged kids like us
Are many,
But few ever admit.
"For sure," I say.

TJ is damaged too.
Stuttering
Once took away his
Every word.
Thoughts interrupted
For years,
Until seventh grade
When he overcame it
Through speech therapy.
But the bullying destroyed him.
His every bit of confidence,
Gone!
I found him with a gun
Loaded and ready
At his house.
Parents gone,

His dad's gun in hand.
He wanted to end it
Even though his stuttering
Was ending and
Only appeared when nervous.
But he was already tormented.
Damage done
By emerging teens that can
Suffocate you
With hate.
And it continued
Through freshman year.
Entitled boys
In two-hundred-dollar shoes
And three-hundred-dollar belts,
Trying to boost their confidence,
Struggling with their insecurities.
They tortured TJ with words.
The gun was taken
In my hands
To never be used,
Never to be spoken of,
Our secret.
We hold each other's secrets.
True friendship is a vault.

"We should hang out sometime," says Audrey.
TJ and I look at each other,
Puzzled.
What do girls do when they hang out?

"Sure" is my reply.
TJ nods his head in agreement.
Audrey finishes her strawberries.
Whispering onlookers
Stare with their
Judgmental eyes.
I hate high school rumors.
Drama that makes no sense
And never does anything
But ruins someone's soul
And crushes their confidence.
"We're going to Bridges after school," I say.
"Bridges?"
"It's a coffee shop that we chill at," I reply.
"Sounds good," says Audrey.
"Good music and coffee," I continue.
"We can give you a ride," says TJ.
Audrey shifts in her seat.
Pause.
"I'll just meet you there," she says,
"I have to meet with a teacher."
"We can wait," says TJ.
Uncomfortable.
Too much too soon.
"No, that's cool. We'll meet you there," I say,
Giving TJ a look to back off.
Audrey relieved,
Bell rings,
The savior of
Uncomfortable silence.

TWENTY-ONE

TJ drinks it black.
I take coffee with cream,
Like Mom always did.
Mom let me drink coffee
In eighth grade.
It seemed to calm me
For some reason,
Unknown to anyone,
But sometimes we need to
Leave unknowns alone.

TJ works on one of the three
AP classes that he's taking.
He doesn't always seem like it, but
TJ is wicked smart,
Scientist smart,
Doctor smart,
Book smart,
But can't put together
A bookshelf to
Save his life.

Other kids filter in,
along with
A few adults.
After school and work,

Getting some
Black magic high.

I chill,
Waiting,
Fixated
On the door
That will
Deliver her.
Fifteen minutes,
Half an hour,
Forty-five,
Hour,
Nothing.
Worried!

TJ is almost done.
He's relaxing into his seat.
I've followed the playlist
In the background:
Iron & Wine,
Gregory Alan Isakov,
Elliott Smith,
Ben Howard,
Damien Rice,
Nick Drake.
They fill my hour,
Fill my mind,
And have helped me survive
Many nights.

She's not coming.
Worried!

Drizzle on the
Coffee shop window,
A sign of spring.
She's standing,
Floating
It seems.
A blurred silhouette.
Her auburn hair
Covered by
A knit hat.
The ends hang down.
Beauty is natural
On her.

Do I go out there?
Do I enter her space?
Do I watch from inside?
Do I retreat?

I go.

"Hey there, you coming in?" I ask.
She shuffles.
"I think...I will," she replies.
No movement.
We stare
At one another

Through drizzle-filled eyes.
I suggest stepping under the awning.
"There's no pressure," I offer.
"I just..." She pauses. "...don't...
Hang out with boys,
Or girls,
Or anyone these days."
The air is cool.
The drizzle causes snow to melt.
A trickle of water sounds as it runs
Down the drain.
"I get it," I say. "I truly do."
I stop there. We both hesitate.
She looks at me and
I feel warm
Drifting into
Her green eyes.
"I want to get to know you," she says.
"Your friend seems alright too."
"He's cool, just a little goofy, but a good guy."
I shuffle my feet.
She stands closer.
"I want to tell you something."
She looks at me seriously.
"Why me?" I say.
"Because I know you're broken too."

I text TJ, "Outside walking with Audrey.
Tell you later."
"K," he replies.

We walk in silence except for passing
Wet tires and running water and
Crackling snowbanks
Shrinking.
I wait patiently,
Giving time.
If she's broken like me,
She needs time
To mold her thoughts
Together into a complete sentence.
"Something happened to me," she starts,
And continues, "Something bad and...
I can't believe I'm even
Telling you this much.
I don't know you...haven't since second grade."
Feet stop.
"Second grade?" I'm confused.
"You don't remember?" she asks.
"I remember very little from then."
She adds, "We used to play at recess
And sat next to each other in Ms. Harman's class."
I start to recall
The girl with long, straight hair
Who would run faster than me
And help me with math
When Ms. Harman wasn't looking.
My voice becomes excited,
For me excited,
Which for others is a normal tone.
"I remember you." I stop and look at

Her face,
That hair.
"I remember you.
That's unreal," I say.
"So, when my dad mentioned that
Your mom died,
I cried for you."
"You lived two blocks over.
We used to ride bikes together." I'm still amazed.
"I left before third grade, when we moved," she says.
"I remember that. I rode my bike by your house
Every day for a month," I say,
And continue, "I didn't know what happened.
I was confused."
"We moved in with my grandma."
She is walking through a puddle, not caring.
"My grandpa died that year, so we didn't want her
To be alone,
And she wouldn't move into our house."
"I'm sorry." I look down.
Death is hard to hold my head up to.
"She died a few months ago."
Audrey's eyes fill,
Tears run from the corners.
"I'm sorry," I say.
It's all I have to offer
Except for knowing how death feels.
"We sold the house and moved back here,
Not too far from where
I lived before,

Where you live," she says.
I stay quiet,
Thinking,
Straining to remember the little girl
With auburn hair that beat me in races and
Hung from playground bars
When we were both pure,
Unbroken.

"So, here's the thing." Audrey stops.
I see her younger eyes,
Those same eyes
From when we were seven.
Eyes don't change.
Memories come back through
Those eyes.
"I had something happen to me,
A boy." She shivers from either
Cold rain or
Memories.
"He did something, and now there are rumors...
And I struggle...
With trusting anyone,
Except my mom and dad...
And maybe
A friend from second grade." She smiles,
A slight smile that
Gives me hope and seems
To give her hope too.

I don't ask her what happened,
I know the rumors.
I don't ask her, "Why tell me?
Why now?"
Because I know how it is
To feel alone in a crowd,
Isolated in your mind,
Trapped,
And the need
For connection,
For "normal,"
If there ever was such a thing.

We find our way back to Bridges and
The smell of roasted beans,
The sound of espresso machines,
Nick Drake hauntingly telling us
Some truth about a black-eyed dog.
TJ looks up. "I finished my AP Calc,
And yours too." He looks at Audrey.
"I've been doing this guy's homework
Since third grade."
Audrey and I laugh
At what we both know
To be our bond,
Connection from second grade.
TJ missed out by a year.

TJ offers, "Can we give you a ride home?"
Audrey looks at me.

"No, I'm going to walk with her
After we have another coffee," I say.
Audrey nods.
"I need to go.
My dad and I watch *Survivor* at seven."
TJ leaves.
Audrey and I both order hot tea for the walk
Home.

We arrive at her doorstep
Three blocks from my house.
I look around.
"I can ride my bike by your house again." I smile,
Then feel awkward,
Uneasy,
Uncool.
"That would be fun when it gets warm," she says.
Frozen by early-March drizzle,
I shiver from cold,
But also with excitement
Of connecting with an old friend.
She turns to walk up
Three concrete steps and
Glances back.
"Stay gold, Ponyboy."
Again, the *Outsiders* reference.
I take the long way home
In hopes of freezing the evening's
Conversations and her beauty
In my head.

TWENTY-TWO

Home.
I walk in.
Dad, paper in hands,
Old-school
In his gathering of news.
"Where were you?" he asks.
"Bridges," I reply.
"Just text me next time," he suggests.
"I will," I say. "I got caught up."
Paper settles across his lap.
"With?" he asks.
"Coffee and TJ obsessing on homework.
He's an animal of intellect."
We laugh.
"And a girl," I hesitantly add.
Dad's paper gets put away, and
He leans in,
Waiting for me to continue.
I'm uncertain what to say.
We've talked about girls once,
We've talked about boys once
Because my dad wanted me to be aware
Of my emotions and sexual interest,
However I felt.
I sit,
Ready to tell him,

In need of answers
About a girl.

"She brightens me," I start,
Then stop.
Sounds corny,
Too much.
Dad smiles.
"Go," he says.
Continuing with the
Unknowing
Of emotions for a girl,
"She just makes me feel..."
Dad nods.
"Whole," I say,
And I sigh.
"The good ones will do that."
Dad's smile fades.
Obviously Mom slipped into
His thoughts,
Together since they were sixteen.
Hardly a day spent apart since,
According to Mom's story,
And Dad's story,
The same story,
Something I want.
"How do I know?" I ask.
"You already said some of
What you need to know,
That she makes you feel whole."

Dad continues as he looks at the mantel,
The fire flickering off Mom's picture
In black and white,
Leaning against a very old tree
In Ireland,
Dad's favorite
Of this worldly,
Earthly,
Amazing woman.
"If it's right,
You will simply want to be
In her presence,
Whether it's walking, talking, or sleeping,
You will look at her and get chills,
And not just in your spine, but your
Hands,
Feet,
Arms,
And chest.
Prepare for the chills
Every time you see her
Because they will make you flush
With energy
And keep you up at night
Thinking about her.
Prepare to talk for hours about
Something meaningful
To you both,
Or prepare to have her
Listen to something

That is
Meaningful
To you and only you,
But she listens from a place of love
And curiosity as to what makes you
Tick,
And breathe...and..."
Dad stops, catches his breath.
He cries
For Mom,
Who made him whole,
And I hug him
Tight,
Trying to keep his
Broken pieces together.
Peter enters and
Stands in front of us both,
Brings his arms around us
And then backs away.
"Mom says hello," he says
And leaves for the kitchen.
Dad and I laugh
With tears in our eyes,
Shattered men trying to feel whole.

TWENTY-THREE

I walk out of my house this morning
Getting to know the concrete a little better,
Longing to be whole, as Dad said.
Looking up,
Audrey stands,
Waiting on a corner.
This is what I had hoped for as
I texted TJ earlier, saying, "Walking to school."
"Yeah, I figured" was his reply.
She's before me,
Audrey with green eyes,
Audrey with auburn hair,
Audrey with kindness in her heart,
Audrey crying.

I don't ask,
Staying silent.
I already know.
Old ghost,
Trauma,
Had to have
Visited her.
I know those
Unexpected tears,
Crying without reason,
Or so we think.

But reasons are many:
Trauma,
Mind fuck,
Screaming insults,
Threats
In your head.
Stealing your worth.

We walk.
Audrey stops.
I wait.
She wipes
Tears
From green eyes
That I want
To swim in.
"I'm a fool," she says.
"Never say that," I reply.
"I'm damaged." More tears,
"You should run...
As far away
From me as you can."
I want to hold her,
Hug her,
At least touch her hand,
But I dare not.
My touch needs to be
Welcomed,
Something Mom taught me long ago.
Dad taught me again last night.

Something that the boy
Who raped Audrey
Should have been taught.
Uncle Kipp should have been taught.
But rapists wouldn't care anyway.
Predators.
"I know your pain," I say.
She pauses, looks deep at me.
I continue, "You know teenagers.
Stories get out."
She doesn't look shocked.
Waits for more.
I give her this: "I am broken too."
She moves forward as I say,
"I'm damaged, and
I would tell you to run,
But I want you to
Run toward me, not away."
I surprise myself.
She smiles.
Sighs.
Eyes lit.
I say, "Maybe we can help each other
Pick up
The broken pieces that have
Shattered?"
She gets closer.
Her breath is like oatmeal
And maple syrup,
Sweet and inviting.

I am still.
"What happened to us from
The playground to now?" She steps back.
"Too much" is all I say.

TWENTY-FOUR

When you find someone that hurts,
And darkness fills their mind,
Demons visit them at night,
Early-morning terrors
Cause sleeplessness,
A shivering existence
Within the dark walls of the
Bedroom,
And intrusive thoughts
Weigh you both down,
You feel less
Alone.
Like you have
An ally
To fight the beast
Within your head.
There is calm in that,
Knowing you have someone
To fight the battle with,
More understanding,
Less judgment.

I ask her, "Do you want to skip?"
She doesn't hesitate. "Yes."
"Wait! Almost forgot, we have
Mr. Johnson's class today."

She nods. "He's cool."
"Yeah, I don't want to disappoint him."
She offers, "How about after his class we leave?"
Agreed.
"I have a special place I want to show you," I say.
"Hmmm...now I'm curious."
"It's a place I go to get lost in thought."
We walk to school and filter in
Among the teenage herd,
A flow of emotions
And
Kids trying to grow up
Too fast.

Mr. Johnson awaits
By his door, greeting students.
He sees us together.
"Glad to see you both," he says, fist-bumping.
I grin.
Mr. Johnson starts class,
Which we all anticipate daily.
"Today, let's discuss that emotion
That baffles us all...
Leaves us either with a
Broken heart
Or a full one.
Nevertheless, a heart beating
In agony
Makes you know you are alive,
Feeling life.

At times, this emotion stirs us up
Into a frenzy that makes our
Heads spin.
Yes, I'm talking about love."
The class giggles
But is interested,
Because to teenagers,
Love means sex
Sometimes,
And love means not being alone
Sometimes,
And love means
Everything
Sometimes.

Mr. Johnson reads from a book,
"'Something in the way she knows
And all I have to do is think of her
Something in the things she shows me.'"
He stops, looks around.
"What does the writer mean?" He pauses
To downed eyes
Studying the floor.
He waits,
A hand,
Audrey.
"Go ahead," Mr. Johnson says.
Everyone looks
At the girl who they judge
For being raped.

Teenage rumors
Saying,
"Whore,"
"Slut,"
"Deserved it."
Audrey speaks. "I think…
That he realizes that
This girl is showing him
The love he never had,
And he realizes that she is
The one…
The one he thinks about
Constantly…
The one…
That he needs to be around
To feel whole."
Audrey stops.
A few giggles.
That word "whole"
Is there again,
Lingering.

Mr. Johnson pauses.
He looks around the class.
He sees and hears the smirks,
Clears his throat.
"Audrey, I think you are right on."
The class silences itself.
"I believe you hit it on the head,
That love can make us feel

Whole.
It's what good love,
Real love, can do,
And it can inspire."
Mr. Johnson looks over
Toward Audrey.
"Thank you!" he says.
"No problem. I adore the Beatles.
I love the song 'Something.'
George is my favorite," says Audrey.
Mr. Johnson smiles
With pride as
He usually has to tell us
Who the writer is.
"A fellow Beatles fan," he says.
More giggles.
"Assignment for today..."
Anticipation.
"Write about love."
A couple of moans
And shifting seats.
"Remember, love is
An emotion that we all have,
So write about anyone
And anything
That you love:
Mom, Dad, siblings, pets,
Significant other,
Or for those that dare,
Write about that person that you love

But they don't know it yet.
Suppressed emotions can be powerful."

I spend the hour
Writing in my journal
And Chromebook.
The journal is for Audrey,
What might be love
someday.
The Chromebook is for
My family,
Dad, Peter,
And Mom,
Who I miss
Beyond comprehension.

Spending the hour
Writing about love,
Something so overwhelming
And mysterious,
Brings me a happiness
That I haven't felt
In a while,
Because with love,
And potential love,
I have hope.
Hope can help me
Hang on.

Mr. Johnson concludes class with:
"'We, unaccustomed to courage
exiles from delight
live coiled in shells of loneliness
until love leaves its high holy temple
and comes into our sight
to liberate us into life.

"'Love arrives
and in its train come ecstasies
old memories of pleasure
ancient histories of pain.
Yet if we are bold,
love strikes away the chains of fear
from our souls.

"'We are weaned from our timidity
In the flush of love's light
we dare be brave
And suddenly we see
that love costs all we are
and will ever be.
Yet it is only love
which sets us free.'"

Mr. Johnson
Gives the class
A once-over,
Checking for emotion,
Because he always says

Poetry, writing
Should bring emotion.

"That is the poem
'Touched By An Angel'
By the great
Maya Angelou.
To have something
So powerful
Like love,
As Ms. Angelou
Has stated,
'To liberate us into life,'
Well, who wouldn't
Want love?
You are all worthy of it."

We leave school
From a side door
Where the cameras
Look one direction
And one only,
And no one goes to
Until there's a concert
Or play.
Escape.

TWENTY-FIVE

We run
To the path
That leads
To liberation
From an institution
That seems to
Drain us
Of our creativity
And often our
Soul.
A brick and
Cement house
Where Judgment rules,
Expectations ruin
Young minds,
Except for Mr. Johnson's class.
He led us to a path
Of processing love.
Thankful!

We walk two miles down a
Gray concrete path,
And when the old oak tree
Displays its beauty,
I stop, smile, and say,
"Are you ready to see
My secret place?"

Audrey looks around.
"That was real?"
"Of course, I'd never lie about a place
Where I go to think, and write,
And sometimes..."
I pause, losing thought as the
March sky
Glows off her hair that
Falls gently
Across her shoulders,
Her pearl-colored skin
Leading to those eyes
That transfix me.
Speechless.
She smiles, shoves me.
"Hey, snap out of it.
Are you losing blood to
Your brain?"
I feel heat in my face.
Blushing, I'm caught.
"See that tree?" I ask,
Pointing to the oak.
"That's my tree."
"I want to see your tree up close," Audrey says,
Nonjudgmental of my claim.
"It's been mine since I was twelve," I say,
And then gently offer her my hand.
She takes it.
The first time
We touch,

Soft, unassuming,
Natural.
"I come here to escape,
And beyond that tree is a creek
That no one seems to know about,
Or at least forgot about."

We walk through the field,
High prairie grass
Where flowers will bloom
In a matter of weeks
And smell wild,
Natural.
Real.

The wetness below our feet
From snowmelt
And rain
Feels right.
We should have to
Work to see beauty.
It should not be
Easy to get to.
It must be earned.

Still holding hands,
No intentions
Except to touch,
To feel
Something,

Anything,
But pain.

The oak tree
Stands tall,
Unwavering,
Steady,
Strong.
We stay silent,
Looking up
At its might,
Then she suggests
Without words
That we see if we can
Wrap ourselves
Around the tree
Without letting go
Of our hands.
Grasped tight,
We move in
Opposite directions,
Only to attempt a
Connection.
The oak is too massive.
We laugh,
Faces against bark,
Still holding on,
Her right hand,
My left,
We pull back together.

Looking into her eyes,
I can almost see
My reflection,
And we stop,
Smile,
And I gently guide her
Through a wooded path.

"It's down here," I say,
And we step over downed wood
Without letting go.
I trust her,
She trusts me,
At least she must
To stray away from society
To an escape where
No one goes.

High in the spring,
The creek is rushing
From the snowmelt.
The rocks are covered,
But my sanctuary is secure.
A leveled tree
Where my back has rested
For several years,
And the woods have
Heard my cries,
My pain,
My secrets.

She breaks the silence.
"This place is peaceful."
She walks closer to the creek.
"I can see why you come here.
It's like another world,
An escape from reality."
She understands immediately
Without hesitation
Because we feel
Similar pain.

Audrey sits against the downed tree.
I watch the slow tears work their way
Down her face.
I sit with her,
Against her,
Shoulder to shoulder,
Warmth.
"Do you want to tell me?" I offer.
She wipes her eyes
With her sweater sleeve,
Those green pools
I've come to love,
And nods.
I wait.

She starts her story while
Staring at the creek.
The flowing water allows
Thought to become deep.

I've experienced it for years.
"My friend asked me to go to a party,
And I really didn't want to because the
Guy who was throwing it had a reputation."
She swallows.
I stare at the water.
I wonder if our eyes
Focus on the same spot.
I am
Mindful of her words,
Each one,
Every emotion.
She continues, "I went with her, you know.
The whole
Peer pressure thing is real."
We chuckle in agreement.
"So I went, and when I got there,
She disappeared
With her boyfriend, even after we agreed
Not to leave each other's side.
She lied,
So I basically stood there,
Not really talking with anyone
But drinking from the tap.
The beer was flowing because
With each cup,
My anxiety went further away,
And I don't drink."
I wait,
Knowing that the story is about to

Unfold
Into a tragedy,
Like so many stories do.
"This guy starts talking to me,
Asking me to help him bring
More beer up from the basement
As he guides my arm.
I remember a few
Glowing stares
From girls snickering, but it's hazy.
Next thing I know..."
Her breathing increases,
Her fists clench,
Tears fall down her cheeks.
Audrey continues, "I'm on a basement floor with
His fucking hands
All over me.
I started to scream, but he put a
Hand over my mouth.
I tried to kick because even though
I was drunk,
I knew what was happening,
But he was strong,
Too strong, and he
Pinned my arms
And laid his weight on my
Stomach and chest.
I couldn't breathe,
I couldn't move,
I felt helpless."

Audrey leans her head into me,
Her hair soft against my cheek.
I hold her gently, safely.
She continues, "He finished,
And then got up like
Nothing happened,
Like he just thought it was
Part of the night,
A door prize,
And he walked upstairs,
Never looking back
As I lay crying on the cement floor."
She rises up and turns to look at me.
"That fucking rapist said I wanted it.
His friends said I wanted it,
Girls at the party said...
Fucking other girls
That should know better...
Said I wanted it.
They all lied, and it
Couldn't be proven,
So he walked."

I'm crying now.
Audrey holds me.
Both of our tears are
Now on her sweater,
Lying together.
Tears of victims
Without any justice.

Our only justice
Was finding each other.

"I started getting harassed,
People saying I was trying to ruin
This guy's life by
Falsely accusing him,
Being told I was a drunk,
Or my shirt and pants were
Too tight, inviting him.
I was called a tease,
A whore,
Ridiculed like I was nothing,
Less than human.
I became suicidal and
Downed some pills,
Cut my wrists,
Anything to kill my pain.
My dad found me.
He saved me,
And that was enough.
We moved."
Audrey pauses and looks at me.
"You know, I still scrub
Myself so hard with soap
In the shower in hopes
Of washing the filth off me.
I just feel
Dirty.
I feel him."

I do know.
I know about
Wanting to kill yourself,
To kill the pain,
To wash off the filth.
I know about being violated,
Raped,
Like you are less than human.
I know about suffering,
Guilt, and shame.
What I don't know about
Is having so many people know.
The tormenting from peers,
The humiliation.
I scream at the water, "Fuck them!"
I stand. "Fuck all of them. You're…"
I wipe my mouth on my sleeve.
"You're amazing, more than amazing, and…
Fuck!"
I fall to my knees, and
Audrey crawls next to me and
Holds me tight.
"I'm so sorry that happened to you,"
I say softly in her ear.
Her auburn hair tickles my lips.
We hold each other and cry
By a creek that has felt, heard, and
Seen my tears,
And now it has Audrey's.

The trees hold secrets,
As does the running water.
They hold our pain close
And our dreams and fears.
And sometimes,
If we're lucky,
The wind comes and takes
Those fears away.

"I want to hear your story."
Audrey takes more of
My tears on her sleeve.
I want to share,
I do, but only TJ knows,
Only Uncle Kipp knows.
Am I ready for Audrey to know?
"I'm not sure...I mean...it may be hard to hear," I say.
"It always is, if we're honest," she replies.
Ghosts seem to want to come out
Along the creekside today.
She adds on, "I know you have pain too.
I can see it.
You carry it like I do,
In your eyes and shoulders.
We depressives can read each other."
She smiles,
And then she does something unexpected,
But what seems natural.
She gently kisses me,
A softness that I have never felt.

If only for a few seconds,
Her kiss told me I would be okay,
That I could open up
And share my secrets too,
My pain.

I start, "We took a family trip
To New Mexico to see my mom's family.
My mom was incredible, by the way.
She was our rock,
So tough and gentle at the same time.
She kept us all together,
Our heads held high.
She's the reason Peter is so strong
And recognizes his abilities,
Not his disabilities."
I stop, and Audrey takes her
Stare from the creek
Back to me.
"I haven't told you about Peter yet.
You will meet him soon and understand."
"I remember him," she says.
She smiles and looks back toward the creek.
Its rushing water calms us both,
As if it's taking some pain away within the current.
"After arriving, my uncle Kipp suggested
Taking me for a hike.
Mom and Dad were fine because at the time,
I looked up to my uncle, a veteran, an outdoors guy
Who would disappear for days or even weeks

In the mountains
And come back with stories of
Facing mountain lions and bears.
He seemed like what a man should be."
This is the most I've talked about Kipp.
I had told TJ a few stories
About the rape, but nothing more.
I continue with the grasp of
Audrey's hand in mine,
The feel of her touch
Pure comfort.
"I went to the mountains with him that day.
It was an out-of-the-way trailhead.
We had to drive two hours to get there.
After we hiked for a while, my legs were jello.
Keep in mind I was
Only twelve, and then
Uncle Kipp came up behind me."
My fist hits the dirt ground.
Audrey moves closer, never taking
Her eyes away from the water.
"He started to kiss me and hold me tighter.
I fought.
I knew it was wrong.
It wasn't like when my dad gave me a
Kiss goodnight or hugged me,
Or when Mom hugged me.
This felt dirty."
Tears fill until the creek
Blends with my eyes,

Blurred, anxious vision.
"Dirty," I repeat.
"He held me down on the ground and then
Raped me.
I was just a little kid."
A sudden flow of adrenaline
Fills my veins.
"I was just a fucking kid!"
I scream to the treetops.
"I fucking hate him.
He took everything.
Innocence,
Youth,
Confidence,
Self-worth,
Dignity.
He took away
My reason
To live.
Everything!"

Audrey leans in,
Puts her head against my chest, and
through broken words says,
"Maybe...he brought you...to me."
I understand immediately
What she means.
For both of us
To find each other
After so many years.

To share ourselves
And my sacred place.
Maybe she's right.
Maybe our tragedies,
Our trauma,
Brought us
Together.

"Did he ever do anything else?" she asks.
I throw a stone
Into the creek
Where it will lie
On the bottom
Until it erodes.
"He did," I say softly.
Head drops.
It's something even TJ
Doesn't know,
A deeper secret.
"He did it again before we
Went back home,
This time
In my grandma's house.
Mom and Dad took Grandma and Grandpa
Shopping, along with Peter.
I hugged my mom hard that day,
But she thought I wanted to
Stay with Uncle Kipp,
As if he was mentoring me.
She couldn't have known,

Dad couldn't have known,
So it happened again.
I wanted to die."

"Have you seen him since?" asks Audrey.
"He came for my mom's funeral," I reply,
And continue,
"The moment I saw him,
Something set off
Inside me,
Like it all came back.
I panicked and ran
Away from the gravesite,
Not even saying goodbye to Mom.
I wanted to kill him.
TJ wants to kill him."
"He knows?" she asks.
I nod.
"And he wants to commit murder on
Your behalf?" she adds.
I nod.
"That's a good friend."
I smile through hurt teeth,
Clenching.
Revealing that much pain
Causes everything to hurt.

We walk out of the woods
Past the oak,
Feeling bark on our fingertips,

And through the tall grass,
Back to the concrete path
Leading to a concrete world,
Where secrets will remain
To haunt us.

TWENTY-SIX

Holding hands to
My house feels
Secure.
Such a simple
Gesture makes me
Leave this
Troubled world
Behind.
I've found a reason
To smile.

Arriving at my front porch,
I say, "You want to meet Peter and my dad?"
She agrees but with some hesitance,
And I know right away,
Even after we shared our
Darkest secrets,
That she still can't fully
Trust me, a boy.
I also struggle with her,
A stranger, a human.
Trust takes time,
Enhanced by actions,
And builds slowly.
She takes one step, then another,
And arrives at my door.

When I open it,
My dad is in the living room
Trying to do some form of yoga
From a video.
Peter beside him
Lying in Savasana.
Not what I was expecting.

"Hey," Dad says without looking up
From Downward Dog.
Peter still relaxed.
"Dad, I have someone I want you to meet."
And just as he is moving to a yogi squat,
He looks up. "Oh, I'm sorry."
Rising to his feet.
"I didn't realize Dylan was bringing
Someone home. Nice to meet you."
Audrey smiles her lovely way.
It's one of the things
I'm starting to become transfixed by,
Her smile, that
Masks pain.
"I hate to stop you from yoga," she says.
"Oh, it's okay," says Dad, and then
He chuckles. "I'm horrible at it...
Dylan and his mom are the experts,
And Peter seems to enjoy one position
And one position only."
We all laugh.

"This is Audrey," I say and hear a strange
Higher-pitched tone release
From my throat.
Dad grins, Audrey smiles at me,
Obviously new territory
And excitement on my end.
"It's nice to meet you," says Dad.

"Peter," I say quietly.
Nothing.
"Would you like to meet someone?"
Nothing.
"Come on, buddy," says Dad.
Peter raises his index finger to
Indicate giving him a moment.
Then he rises, rubs his eyes.
"Mom was telling me something
Important, and I needed to let her
Finish before she had to go."
Envy.
Peter rolls to one side,
Pops up,
And comes to me,
Hugging my rib cage
Until I feel like it might crack.
"Mom says hello
And for you to stay in school."
Audrey and I look at each other,
Busted by Peter and
Apparently my mom.

Peter moves directly in front
Of Audrey, looks up to see her face.
"Hello, I am Peter." He extends his hand
For her to shake, and she does.
Peter lets go while looking at
Audrey's eyes in depth,
Like the first time I saw them.
"You have really green eyes,
Pretty, like a rock I found.
Remember the rock, Dylan?
The one from Lake Michigan
That is green like Audrey's eyes?"
At first, I stand unsure how Audrey
Will react to Peter,
And then my trust, maybe love,
Grows quickly.
"I'd like to see that rock if you have it, Peter.
Can you show me?" asks Audrey.
Peter leaves quickly toward his room.

"Have a seat," says Dad and then adds,
"Would you like something to drink?"
Audrey looks at me as if to ask,
Is this okay?
I smile back, taking her hand
To silently tell her, "*Yes.*"
As Dad sees the gesture, he smiles.
"How about tea?" he says.
"Tea would be great," says Audrey.
Her hair falls over her shoulders and down her

Back, leaving me entranced for a moment
With how straight it is, and how the color
Is so natural.
Audrey is natural.

Dad arrives with tea.
Audrey lets it sit
On her lap,
Not letting go
Of my hand,
And it feels
Secure.

"Peter must be shuffling through some things
To get the rock," says Dad as the noise from
Peter's room heightens.
"I remember Peter," says Audrey.
Dad looks amused.
I say, "Really?"
"Yeah, I remember him from Harris."
Harris Elementary was our school
From so long ago.
"That's so wild," I say.
"He's older than you, right?" says Audrey.
"You know each other?
You know Peter?"
Asks Dad, leaning in a little more.
"Dad, we found out we knew each other in
Second grade.
Audrey moved that year."

"That's amazing." Dad sips some tea.
"And how did you meet again?"
I'm about to speak up and for a moment
Want to stop the questions from Dad
Because maybe questions will lead
To unwanted memories, but then
Audrey adds, "My parents moved us at the
End of my second grade year
To a different part of town.
We recently came back."
She seems to
Like the conversation, and that
Dad is interested.

Peter comes rushing
Out from his bedroom
In front of Audrey
With a green rock
That has been smoothed
By the Great Lakes.
He places it next to Audrey's
Eyes while she calmly sits still.
"Yep, a perfect match," says Peter.
"Your eyes are pretty like the rock."
Audrey smiles. "Thanks, Peter."
"I found your eyes..." Peter rolls the rock
Between chubby fingers
And continues, "...in the sands
Of the beach,
Where everything is beautiful."

Audrey and I glance at each other.
Mr. Johnson would consider Peter
A poet, and probably read his words
About beauty at the start of class.
Audrey smiles. "Peter, you are so thoughtful."
Peter hands her the rock. "You should have your eyes."
Then he looks at the clock. "My show is on."

Dad sits back,
Looks tired.
Not from work.
Not from yoga.
Only the type of tired
That loss can bring,
Crying can bring,
Grieving can bring.
The type of tired
That makes you weak
From thought,
From love,
From regret,
From guilt,
From despair,
From memory.

We talk with Dad about
School and walking
The path
That leads us to telling stories,
But we lie about when

We walked and where we walked
And what was said.
All he needs to know
Is that we walked.
And again, as Dad is
Sharing conversation,
I can see how he longs
To walk with the person
He loves and share secrets
In a secret place,
And then he stands and leaves,
Tears starting.

"Is he okay?" asks Audrey.
I nod. "He is, but I think...
Maybe seeing you...
Us together...
That he misses my
Mom even more."
Audrey nods and grips my hand.
"I sometimes think..."
I clear my throat.
"...that I lost a mom, but he
Lost his love."
Audrey moves closer,
Her hip next to mine.
"Love like that has to be
Devastating
To lose," she says.

I walk her home,
The cool wind against us,
Making our cheeks red
And our hands that don't
Hold one another
Cold, and I know
My other hand will soon
Join in on the chill,
As it will be released from hers.
I suddenly want to never
Let go.

Half a block away,
We stop and linger,
Looking into Peter's rock
That Audrey holds in her palm.
"I want you to hold this and
Have my eyes with you
All the time," she says.
I take the rock as our palms
Stay locked in place,
Holding it together for a moment.
I lean in, only a short way,
Not forcing it, but hoping.
And she comes the rest of the way.
The softness of her lips
Touches mine, and we seemingly
Kiss to end the day.
We have combined
Our stories,

Our hurt,
Into one another.
Release,
And there are
More tears,
Too many for a day,
But like Mom always said,
"Don't judge your tears."
We both wipe our eyes,
And then I watch her walk away.
She turns and smiles.
"Stay gold, Ponyboy."

TWENTY-SEVEN

I enter the house.
Dad sits staring
At the fire
And doesn't look up.
I sit quietly, close.
"Dad, you okay?"
"I'm sorry, buddy."
"No worries."
"I was lost in thought." He smiles.
"Did you get Audrey home?" Dad asks.
"Yeah, she lives about three blocks away."
"Sweet girl," he says,
"I can tell you really like her."
Smiling,
Glowing.
"I do," I reply,
"I just..." Stopped by fear.
"Yeah?" Dad seeks more.
"I just...don't want to blow it.
 I want her to like me back."
"Well, I'm no expert." He stares back at the fire,
Places his hands together.
"Your mom and I got together when we were your age,
So I wouldn't think about it too much.
Just let it happen
Naturally and enjoy each other.
Keep taking your walks,

Hold hands, talk to one another
Until your mouth is dry,
And try to never lose interest,
Never judge."
Then he cries.
I hug my dad
Harder than I have ever hugged him before
As he weeps for my mom,
His wife,
Companion,
Lover,
And I can feel his pain
Against mine.
"And son..."
I wait.
"...just help keep each other in school." Dad smiles.
"Deal," I say.

TWENTY-EIGHT

Green grass showing.
Summer is in the corners
Of my mind.
April is here,
Spring break is here,
Audrey is here,
Holding my hand,
Taking walks,
Letting everything happen
Naturally.

Dad, "Let's go see your grandparents over break."
Me, "I kinda want to stay home this break."
Dad, "Dylan, I know why you want to stay."
Me, "I just...worry about her."
Dad, "Why so worried?"
Me, "I'm her only friend, and I guess TJ is too."
Dad, "I get it, but it's also good to give each other space."
Me, "Space?"
Dad, "Well, sometimes it's good to be away from each
    other."
Me, "Why?"
Dad, "To see how much you miss each other."
Me, "Doesn't sound worth it."
Dad, "Maybe you've got a point.
Time will tell you many things,
Maybe it's telling you already that

She's a rare find,
Like your mom."
Me, "So, I don't have to go?"
Dad, "I'll get back to you."

Last day of class,
Audrey isn't at school.
She texts to say she will be late,
But it's third period,
Mr. Johnson's class,
And we both agreed
To never miss Mr. Johnson's class.
Worried!

I'm worried because
Two nights ago,
As we walked under the
Moonlight,
Crisp air on our faces,
I suddenly stopped moving
In a long moment of silence
After she talked about
Her depression,
And how she's been having
Nightmares,
And I said something
I've only said to Mom, Dad, and Peter,
And thought about with TJ.
"I love you."
I shocked myself

With my words,
But they just came out,
Stormed out
Of my mouth.
And I didn't say it
To hear it back,
I just wanted her to know,
Because Mom always said,
"Love can heal pain."
And Audrey is in pain.
She did say it back,
Softly,
In her sweet voice,
And her words ring
In my ears.
"I love you, Dylan.
Thanks for finding me. More importantly,
Thanks for helping me find myself."

Mr. Johnson, "Where's Audrey?"
As I enter.
"I'm not sure." Worried.
"She said she'd be late."
Voice jittery.
Mr. Johnson, "I'm sure she will show."
Pats my shoulder and pulls me aside.
"Let me tell you something."
He stops himself as other students filter in.
"Love, which I believe you two have, will hurt
Sometimes."

I'm silent, waiting for more.
He continues, "When you're not together,
You will feel like a part of you is missing."
I nod because he's right,
A part of me is empty,
Hollow,
When she's not around.
Perhaps it's really love.

Mr. Johnson has become an ally,
Someone we talk to in after-school
Gatherings, where we feel
Normal
And learn from him
About life.
He's the first teacher to understand.
The first to name our
Depression and anxiety
And talk about it openly, like it's part of
Us, because it is.
He has similar darkness,
And through describing his pain,
Our pain becomes more real,
Normal.

I walk in and sit down,
Glancing at Audrey's
Empty chair.
That's me,
Empty.

Mr. Johnson starts class.
"Listen closely," he says.
Plays a song,
The Avett Brothers,
"No Hard Feelings."
The song ends.
A student, Lilly, cries
And then laughs
Because of unexpected tears.
Her friends laugh with her.
I think of Audrey.
Mr. Johnson says,
"'When my body won't
Hold me anymore and it finally
Lets me free,
Where will I go?'"
Pauses for effect.
"What are your thoughts?
And Lilly, never try to hide your tears
Or laugh at them, because there's meaning
In them.
All tears have meaning."
Lilly nods her head in agreement
And adds, "My grandpa died last summer.
That song reminded me of him. He was a veteran
And struggled a lot after the war."
Mr. Johnson nods. "Powerful, Lilly."

The class is silent.
Mr. Johnson lets it happen.

Perhaps everyone is thinking
About meaning behind their tears.
My tears bleed with
Grief,
Sadness,
Loss,
Hurt,
Violation.

I slowly,
Passively,
Raise my hand.
Something I never do.
I'm not bold
Like Audrey.
Beautiful
Like Audrey.

"Dylan," says Mr. Johnson.
"The floor is yours."
"I think the singer is contemplating death," I start,
"Trying to understand
The pain we feel...
The love we feel...
And the sacrifices that life brings...
And what we learn from all
The emotions life offers.
Possibly, it's about
Forgiving our enemies,
The ones that hurt us,

And how hurt
And the anger and torment it causes
Does more harm than good
Because anger fills your head and
Can steal your smile,
Leaving you with nothing but resentment,
Usually towards yourself."
I look up after losing myself
In thought.
The class is staring,
I'm a little dizzy,
Lilly is crying again.
Mr. Johnson breaks the silence.
"Dylan, I don't think any more needs to be said.
Well done."
The class is still silent.
"Now, take that emotion and go write."
Mr. Johnson sits and writes with us.
Perhaps he has some reconciliation of his own.

TWENTY-NINE

The counselor pulls me
Out from fourth hour.
My counselor,
Don't know her name,
Always more concerned with
ACT scores
And college entrance exams
Than depression or anxiety.
Following close behind, she is
Quiet.
It has to be the check-in
For skipping class.
They will ask why.
I'll say, "I'm grieving the loss of my
mom."
They will excuse it and
Leave me alone.
It's happened before.
It seems grief is a subject
That pushes people away.
I think all tough subjects,
The ones that matter,
Always do.

Arrive at Student Services,
The dean is there.

I have no weed, so
Quit eyeballing me.
That thought stays
In my head.
Mom would be proud.
I sit in the counselor's office,
Fidget spinners all over the table,
Bacteria-holders,
"Fecal magnets," the other kids say.
I move back a little.
"Dylan, Audrey's dad just called." The counselor
Looks down.
I sit forward and want to say,
"It was only a kiss."
But refrain.
Silence is my defense.
"She's in the hospital."
The counselor looks up at me,
Pauses.
"She took a bottle of pills.
Her dad found her unconscious."
I cry immediately,
Like the tears were just
Hanging on the edge,
Waiting to fall from
My eyes.
Head in hands,
Fist slams on the table.
"Fuck!"
Fecal fidgets fly.

"Is she...dead?" I ask.
Another death,
Another loss
Of someone I love.
My own death drifts
In front of my thoughts
For a moment.
"No," the counselor says,
Then adds, "I'm sorry, I should
Have said that first."
"Fuck!" I scream again.
She sits back like I might
Attack.
"Dylan, just breathe."
"Don't give me that shit.
Not now. Not when death
Is so close."
"She is okay. They pumped
Her stomach
And saved her,
But she is hospitalized until
she's better."
"Better?" I look up.
I see fallen fidgets
And want to stomp them,
Put them out of their
Shitty misery
From teenage fondlings.
I continue, "What does
'Better' mean?"
"She's in the emergency room.

Her dad wanted you to know
Because you are on the visitors list."

I abruptly leave
For Audrey,
Who still breathes.
I need her to breathe
For me, and I will
Breathe for her.
She's my oxygen,
I will be hers.

She suffers
In her mind
Because her body
Was violated
Without consent,
Without compassion
Or passion.
She suffers
In her mind
Because the darkness,
The memory,
Is too real,
Like a movie
Playing over and over.
A horror film.
The gore is your
Thoughts
Killing you
Slowly.

THIRTY

TJ is waiting for me
Outside Student Services.
The dean approaches.
"His dad is getting him," says the guy
In pointy dress shoes and too tight pants,
Trendy haircut and trimmed beard.
TJ says, "Not anymore.
I'm taking him.
His dad knows."
"Well, you need to be called out.
Did your parents…"
We walk away before
The dean can finish.
"They will," says TJ.
I think the dean's pants are gonna split.
TJ took charge,
Like he can.

His car is parked in the
Front of the school,
Idling and ready, warm and
Capable.
"That fucker was getting into our business," TJ grunts.
I nod.
"Can't stand him," says TJ.
"Doesn't matter," I muddle.
"Yeah, well, he better step off."

TJ is talking tough,
Almost like he's happy to be
Protecting me, taking care of me.
"Thanks for taking me," I say.
"Who else would take you?
Your lazy ass doesn't have a car."

Light mist on the window,
Houses pass like a blur.
Life is passing like a blur.
Death is becoming too clear.

My thoughts scream at me.
Why didn't I go to her house?
Why didn't I stop her?
Why did she want to leave me?
Doesn't she love me?
It's all my fault
For allowing myself to get close
To someone so broken.
To anyone!
Fuck you, thoughts!

We arrive at the hospital,
Walk through the doors.
Dad comes and hugs me.
Behind him, Mr. Johnson, who
Hugs me too.
Two men I respect
And care about.

Then I am lifted
By Peter as he
Wraps his arms
Around me,
So hard I'm on my
Tiptoes,
Almost dangling,
And he whispers,
"Mom is right here."

These men,
All of them,
Dad,
Mr. Johnson,
TJ,
Peter,
Walk with me,
Behind me by only steps.
Close enough to offer me their
Strength
Because they know
That I need their
Courage
More than ever to fight the
Battle
In my mind,
And be there for
Audrey.

So we walk
Like a
Platoon
Going into
War.

Waiting room,
Audrey's parents
Feeling pain
Like I saw
When we waited
For Mom to die,
To get the final word.
Except Audrey isn't dying,
She just wanted to,
And I know that feeling
Only too well.

"Thank you for being here,"
Says Audrey's dad.
Her mom hugs me.
"You are good for her," she says.
She must see the guilt in my eyes,
Trying to reassure me
That this isn't my fault.
The human body has
An endless supply of tears.
They drain us
Like emptying a sink.

We wait silently.
Doctor approaches.
"She's okay." She starts
The way one should start
A conversation when death
Is in question,
So near.

"Is this family?" she asks.
Audrey's dad glances over,
Replies, "If they are here,
concerned, they are family."
The doctor continues,
"Her blood pressure is stable.
We are moving her to the
Psychiatric unit soon."
"How long will she be there?"
I hesitantly ask.
"One week," says the doctor.
She leaves,
Escorting Audrey's parents
Back to see her.

Of course one week.
One week is all kids ever get.
At school, when a kid disappears
For one week when it's not vacation,
We all know where they went.
One week of counseling.
One week of talking about not killing yourself.

One week of convincing them why you shouldn't kill
    yourself.
One week of going on meds that they think will cure you.
One week of feeling insane.
One week of cafeteria trays and stale food.
One week that Audrey will be away from me.
Feeling selfish,
But I know I can help her more
Than strangers with name tags.

Audrey's parents return.
Her mother cries.
Her dad approaches.
"Dylan, she asked for you.
Head on back, but...
Be aware that she doesn't
Look good."
My thoughts are, *Thank you for*
Allowing me to see your daughter, and
What the fuck did you think she'd look like?
Mom would have been happy
That I kept that deep within.
I know that's the fear in my head, so I simply nod,
Then take the long walk back to the small curtained area
Where they are keeping the girl that I may
Be in love with.

And as I enter
To see her tired eyes
And gentle smile,

I realize that I am
Dark enough
To see her light.

I go immediately to her,
Lean in and kiss her softly,
Much like our first kiss.
And she holds my face
As I shed a tear on her cheek
And whisper, "I love you,"
As our minds seem to combine,
And she says, "I love you too."
And her tears flow with mine
And I say, "I don't want you to feel this life
Without me. Your pain is mine,
And mine is yours,
And together we can make it."
And there she is,
Her auburn hair and pale skin
And her green eyes and warmth.
There she is, back in my arms.
She's returned to life right
Before me, and she sets my mind free,
And she whispers, "I'll be here for you,
Always, and I'll never try to leave this world again.
You do the same."
A contract for life.

From behind, I hear my dad and Peter.
"Audrey, you gave us a scare," says Dad.

"We are here for you, so let me know what you need."
Then Dad does something I don't expect.
He reaches for her hand and says, "I never had a daughter.
Dylan and Peter's mom always wanted one, and so
I guess you are my daughter, so take care of yourself."
Then Dad turns as he starts to well up in tears
That a father sheds for broken children.
Peter steps up, standing straight and
Strong,
Directly at the foot of Audrey's bed, and
Says with
Assurance,
"You are then my sister, and I love you.
And also, Mom says that
You will be okay.
You just need to let us help you.
And when you are better,
You can come and talk to her with me."
Peter leaves.
Dad follows.
Audrey is smiling, beautiful, tender.
"Well, I guess I've been adopted."
We both laugh, and I lay my head against hers.

"There are my kids." Mr. Johnson enters.
We smile, adopted again.
"Well, you are all my kids, my only kids."
"Well, damn," says Audrey,
"My family just keeps growing."
Mr. Johnson stands next to me,

His hand on my shoulder.
"I am here for you both when you need me."
And then he looks directly at Audrey.
"I've been here, right where you are, so I get it.
Life leads us on a pretty thorny, rocky path at times,
One that we struggle to wrap our heads around
And one that is dark, and overwhelming,
Lonely.
The loneliness is the hardest part.
Being lonely when
You're with people that love you is torture
Because you feel like you should be happy,
But that's depression.
The little, dark fucker
Wants to steal your smile.
It wants to ruin you
Into thinking you're nothing
And life isn't worth living.
But it is, so use your darkness and pain
To find beauty and reason in your suffering
And then go do something extraordinary with the life
That you have been given."
Another lesson from a man who seems to know
About life.
Mr. Johnson hands Audrey a book,
The Collected Stories by Grace Paley.
"For your week away," says Mr. Johnson,
And then he walks out.

I don't stop holding Audrey's hands
And continue to rest my head against hers,
Wanting her to feel my love,
Savor it and keep it in her thoughts
All week during her recovery.

"I don't want to stay here," she says.
"I don't want you to either." I look at her lips
And want to kiss them again.
"I want to be with you, and now I've been adopted."
We laugh.
"I can take care of you," I say,
"I'll be with you."
"I know you will.
I'm done wanting to kill myself."
I sit up and look at her.
"No, I don't think you are.
I know I'm not."
She looks at me with a wrinkled brow.
"I don't understand," she says.
"We both have had something..." I pause.
"...horrible happen to us,
And we have depression.
I'm just saying,
We will want to
Die over and over again...
The difference is not doing it
Because we have each other."
She agrees with a nod and
Pulls me in for a kiss.

"It sounds to me, Audrey,
That Dylan will help you
Better than anyone in this hospital can."
Audrey's dad is directly behind me,
Hand on the same shoulder that Mr. Johnson's was.
He heard everything.
"Do you think so too?" he asks.
"Yes, I think we need to be together.
He understands me and
What I've gone through more than anyone."
And with that, her dad turns to leave,
Saying, "Then I'll let them know
I'll be taking you home."

THIRTY-ONE

A day later,
Audrey stands before me
At her front doorstep,
Waiting for a walk
Down the path
To the creek
Where secrets
Are shared
And held
Close.

Blue sky
Covering the field,
Flowers lead to the oak
Where we pause
To wrap our bodies
Around its trunk
And then each other,
Holding close,
Not wanting to let go.
I fall
Into her eyes.

She smiles,
Releasing my hand,
Releasing my heart
A little more

To love her,
And leads me to the creek
Where we go shoeless
In the moving water,
Where it takes our fears
Away downstream.
And Audrey comes to me,
Audrey with the hair,
Audrey with the eyes,
Audrey with the wounded soul,
Audrey with the strength
To keep moving forward.
She gently takes me
Into her arms and
Kisses me.
Meaningful,
Like our last
Or our first again.
Transfixed.

As we embrace,
Thoughts race.
How I almost lost
Her to something
So traumatic,
Where she only feels
Free,
Released from her pain,
By taking her life.
I pull away.

"Please never leave me."
"I promise," she says.
"If you are going to,
Just tear my heart out now,"
I say as I lean in.
She stops.
"I had a dream about you."
"Oh," I say with a curious smile.
"Not that type of dream," she says, and
We laugh.
"Well, what was it?" I ask.
"We were old, walking a dirt path
That led to a waterfall,
And you held me underneath it
As the water fell over
Wrinkled skin and gray hair
As we smiled and danced."
I can't help myself.
I lean in the rest of the way,
Breaking my rule to let her come the
Rest of the distance,
Excited to take the life
Journey that will lead us
To that waterfall.
A soft kiss.

We walk barefoot back to the oak tree.
"We need to talk about something," says Audrey.
I nod.
"I know that...well...I know we hold hands and kiss

And that you probably want more, and..."
I step back.
She is shaking a little, nervous to talk about sex.
Frightened maybe.
I understand.

"Audrey." I come back to her,
Holding her shaking hands.
"I don't care.
Holding your hand,
Holding you close,
Holding your heart to mine
Is all I care about.
I just want
To be with you."
Audrey's eyes are filled
again, proving our bodies have
Limitless tears
Waiting on the surface to come out.
"How come I didn't find you before I..."
She puts her head into my chest,
Flannel shirt soaking her tears.
"You found me now" is all I say.

THIRTY-TWO

As we walk, she says,
"I have to go see Peter."
"How come?"
"He called me." She smiles.
"Called you?"
"Yeah, he had your phone.
Your name came up, but it
Was Peter inviting me over."
"Well, I guess you better go."

Peter comes out of his room as we enter.
"Hello, Audrey," he says.
Dad says, "You good?"
"Yes, much better." Audrey smiles.
Dad hugs her.
"Remember, we are here
For you, all of us."
"I know." Audrey leans in and hugs him again.
"Okay, are you ready?" asks Peter,
And then he takes Audrey to his room
Where he watches *Star Trek*.
I smile, sitting on the couch.
"He must have invited her for an episode," I say.
"Yeah, he's been talking about it for the past hour.
Does she seem okay to you?"
Dad is concerned.
"Are you okay?"

I nod. "I think so. I just...am scared and don't want
To lose her.
Ever."
"Loss is painful.
It leaves you empty. I have you and Peter,
But I'm lonely without your mom.
She made everything better,
Made me better.
I looked forward to getting up every day
Just to see her."
I wonder for a moment,
When Dad sees Audrey, does it make him
Feel
The loss of Mom even more?
"I also know that loss,
Losing those we love,
Is a part of this life
And why we stay grieving.
I guess what I'm saying, Dylan, is
Hang onto her with all your might."
"I told her I love her," I say.
Dad sits up. "And..."
"She said it back."
Dad grins. "How did it make you feel?"
"It scared the hell out of me," I answer.
"That's love," says Dad. "It will definitely
Scare the hell out of you."

Audrey and Peter
Come back about a half hour later.

We leave, and I walk her home.
For the three blocks, she is silent,
And I wonder if she's feeling ill.
"Are you okay?" I ask.
"I'm good." She stops.
"Your brother is...I'm not sure."
"Obsessed with *Star Trek*," I reply.
"We didn't watch *Star Trek*.
We spoke to your mom."
Surprised.
"Well, what did she say?"
"That I will need to help you soon
Because you will face something
That will require all of your strength."
"Okay, I'm a little freaked out."
I stop walking and look at Audrey.
"Peter came up with that?"
"Dylan, I think Peter is really
Talking to your mom.
He was having a
Conversation with her,
Introduced me, and then we spoke
Through him about you."
I don't know how to feel.
Why can't I talk to Mom?
I try but don't hear anything back.
I'm a little angry,
Not at Audrey or even Peter,
But at Mom for leaving me
And not letting me have

Conversations with her.
I need to tell her
So much.
As Audrey leaves, she says,
"Maybe you just need to believe
A little harder."
I nod, not saying anything.
"Stay gold, Ponyboy," she says.
I walk home and watch
The Outsiders
For the eleventh time.
I want to stay gold.

THIRTY-THREE

It's my first prom.
It took me to senior year
To even want to go.
I ask her because
It seems like the thing to do.
A little cliché for us,
But nevertheless,
Audrey says, "Yes."
I think I just want any excuse
To hold her, so prom is one more.
Audrey laughs and says,
"I'm not getting some little skimpy dress,
And I'm not going to have it sparkle."
I comment, "I wouldn't want it any other way."

I tell her, "I don't want to be like everyone else
And follow some stupid tradition, so
I'm taking you to dinner afterward."
That makes her smile.
"I'll eat a snack to keep me full until then."
TJ is there too,
By himself,
And they ask at the door, "Who is your date?"
TJ replies, "Is that a requirement?"
We all walk in together.
I'm not much of a dancer,

But TJ loves to, so he goes right to the middle
Like no one else is there and starts
Doing some mixture of an '80s dance,
Moshing first, and then the
Robot, and eventually a breakdance.
His body is all over the place, and the other
Kids give him space and laugh
But a few join in.
Audrey pulls my hand to go
Out there to dance with TJ.
I can't resist her smile and persuasion
So I go and fumble through some
Side-to-side move that I invent on the spot.
Audrey moves and sways to the beat,
Her hair swinging from one side of her back to the
other,
And finally, a slow song.

I move closer,
She steps in.
I place my hands
On her back,
Not too low,
Like Dad taught
When he showed me how
To slow dance last night
In our living room
To some singer named
Bryan Adams.
Audrey leans into me,

Our stomachs and
Chests breathing
In unison.
All sound drowns out as
I look into her eyes.
It feels like we are underwater,
Hidden from the rest of the world,
And she says to me, "I love you so much!"
And then we slow our steps,
And I whisper back, "You are now my memory."
Feeling like I just said something completely
Awkward, I move back
Until she pulls me into her again and says,
"I want to be your memory and your present."
"And my future," I add.
I kiss her gently.

I look at my watch, ten o'clock,
I want to go, to show her the surprise.
TJ knows and suggests we leave too.
Audrey is suspicious, but we leave.
She has started to trust riding in a car
With boys again, meaning me and TJ.
Trust is built through time
And actions.

TJ drops us off at the trailhead.
Audrey smiles. "What's going on?"
TJ drives off, giving me a salute and Audrey a fist bump.
"I have a surprise." I take her hand and start walking.

"You've got that smile, where your dimples are just a
Little deeper."
I kiss her hand.
The crossing to the oak tree is just ahead.
Audrey sees the flickering light next to the creek.
Curious, she walks a little faster
In her flowered dress,
The prettiest dress at prom.
We get to the oak tree
Where solar lights have created a path
That leads to the creek.
"What in the world?"
She is glowing
Both by the light and her smile.

When we come to the end of the path
Where the creek is trickling,
A small table
Covered in white cloth
And two chairs sit close to the creek,
A candle in the middle.

Our dads step out,
Along with Audrey's mom,
And Peter, in a tuxedo,
Who left the dance early
So he could be our waiter.
From what I hear, he
Tore up the dance floor
Before we got there.

Audrey's dad had set up a large
Display of solar lights
That glow softly from her skin
And the creek water.
My dad starts to unpack the cooler,
And Peter guides us to our seats
And holds Audrey's chair for her.
Audrey's mom, who plays the guitar,
Starts to strum the softest,
Sweetest music I've ever heard,
Like her instrument is weeping.

"This is amazing," says Audrey.
"I did this for you," I reply.
"But now it's out," she whispers softly,
"They know your secret place."
"Well, it's our secret place," I correct her,
"But it was worth it." I chuckle.
Peter brings us sparkling water,
Pours it in the glasses on the table,
And says, "Ma'am and sir, your first course is coming."
He says it perfectly, just like we rehearsed.
Audrey smiles at Peter. "Thank you so much."
Peter backs up one step and turns
Like Dad practiced with him in the living room.
Dad taught us a lot in the living room.
I lift my glass. "I'd like to make a toast."
I have never given a toast in my life.
Audrey lifts her glass.
"To your dream by the waterfall. May that come true."

Audrey takes a sip and then reaches for my hand,
Warmth,
Soft,
Safe,
And simply says, "Yes."

Then, as her mom continues to play,
Our dads start singing,
Something I don't expect,
Not part of the plan,
But they sing a duet
Of "Love and Some Verses" by Iron & Wine.
It's our song,
Audrey and me,
Being sung by two men
We love,
And the chords
Perfect
By her sweet mother,
With Peter swaying to
A song we shared,
With emotions that we share.

Peter brings over a small salad,
Laying it gently on the table,
And as he pauses,
He can't
Resist anymore and leans
Over and gives me a hug,
And then goes to Audrey and

Does the same but longer,
Saying to her, "Mom says hello."
Then Peter goes next to our dads
And listens to the guitar being played
And the creek water trickling.

Audrey is silent while eating.
Worried that something is wrong,
Maybe something I did or said,
I hesitantly interrupt her thoughts.
"Is everything okay?" I ask.
She looks up, softly smiling.
Every time I see her smile,
It grows my heart like a garden
To know that maybe I'm part of her
Reason for smiling.
"I'm just thinking about how far...
How strange...this journey and
Life is."
I leave my fork on my plate,
Reaching for her hand,
Her fingers becoming familiar within mine.
"I can understand that," I say.
"To have so much taken from me,
From us both, and then to be here
With you, in our secret place, I just feel...
Loved." She strokes my fingers with hers.
"It's our journey now," I say.
She has a delicate look on her face.
Delicate from time that has

Taken its toll
And from hope of a future
All at the same time.
"I don't want you to feel life
Without me," I say.
Audrey's green eyes seem
To enter mine as her stare
Is all I need to confirm
That she feels the same,
And for a single moment,
Single breath,
I wonder, will I always need
Confirmation that she loves me?

Peter interrupts with our main course,
Cheeseburgers that Dad grilled before he came,
With roasted potatoes,
Audrey's favorite meal.
"I think we may have to leave our waiter a tip," says Audrey.
Peter starts laughing and says, "Leave it on the table."
We laugh as our dads gather the dishes.
Audrey's mom packs up her guitar, and then
They all walk toward the oak tree,
Leaving the solar lights and small
Fire that my dad built within a rock ring.
They are all gone, leaving chocolate cake
That I bought at Bridges because it is
Audrey's favorite and she eats it each time
We go there.

I stand and take her hand,
Guide her to where a blanket
Is spread out next to the creekside
And next to the downed log
That we have leaned on each time.
We listen to the wind lift,
The creek run smoothly
Over rocks, and watch a yellow
Moon trickle through the trees.

The night is becoming cool,
So I cover Audrey's shoulders
With an extra blanket.
She leans against me
As we talk quietly about
Our first prom,
How TJ danced,
How her dress was beautiful,
How my shirt and tie blended,
All black,
With a purple flower from Audrey,
Peter's skills as a waiter,
Her mom's serene playing,
And our dads, becoming friends
Through us, finding each other.
Men bonded by broken kids.
And as the stories unfold,
We fall asleep,
Holding each other for warmth.

Waking up two hours later,
Cold from the fire going out,
Red and gray coals remain.
Still, her auburn hair looks
Like it's burning
As it rests on my chest.
Peaceful as she sleeps,
Because when trauma invades
Your every thought
Every waking hour,
Sleep is often your only
Escape.

She lifts her face to mine
And slowly starts to kiss me,
And we come together
Gently on the blanket.
Next to the water running,
Still desperately trying to carry
Our pain with each current of
Liquid over rock,
We do not say anything.
Nothing is needed from our voices as
Our bodies communicate with each other.
And Audrey lets me love her.
Discovering each other,
Our hearts beat close,
Our breath working in unison,
Together,
Natural,

Loving.
The way it should be.

We walk out from the woods,
Stopping to hug our oak tree,
Skipping across the field,
Breaking into a stride,
Laughing,
Joyful.

I walk her home
Down our path
As the sun slowly
Lifts into the morning sky.
We smile as our lives
Seemingly start to
Take on new meaning,
Not without memory,
But maybe with hope.

THIRTY-FOUR

When I come into our house
The next morning,
Exhausted from lack of sleep
But elated with
Everything Audrey,
I find Dad
Awake and broken down,
Slumped in his recliner.
I don't need to look any further
Than his hands
To see the reason.
It's the photo album
That Mom had since high school.
Most of the pictures are of
Mom and Dad
At school dances,
Taking day trips,
Starting a life
Into the unknown.
Looking and feeling
Invincible.
Everything before them.

I have looked through the photos
A thousand times,
Always wanting what they had,

And since Mom died,
Trying to see her younger,
Healthier self.
Longing
For something
To stay connected,
For her to live through pictures.

I sit next to Dad,
Appreciating his emotions.
Never trying to hide them,
Never being a father, like TJ's,
That doesn't believe in men
Showing any feeling.
And dear God,
Absolutely no crying.
"Men don't cry," I once heard TJ's dad
Mutter,
And so I don't go over there that often.
I can't take
Suppressed male emotions,
Insecurity at its best.

"Are you okay?" I ask.
"I just miss her so much."
Dad holds a picture of Mom,
Senior-year skip day,
On a beach at Lake Michigan,
Smiling and eating an ice cream cone.
"I'm not sure I can handle

The pain some days." Dad then adds,
"Sorry."
I look directly at him.
"You don't have anything to be sorry about."
Dad looks up and smiles.
"The person you loved more than anything died.
The person you built a life with is gone.
There's nothing to feel sorry about,
Except that we can't get her back."
Dad wipes his eyes.
"I've shed so many tears these past few months,
I'm surprised
I'm not dehydrated."
We both laugh.
I lie back on the couch and
Look up at the ceiling.
"You're in pretty late, or early
I guess since it's morning," Dad says.
"Yeah, we fell...asleep," I say, grinning.
"Well, I hope you were safe while you 'slept.'"
He uses air quotes when he says "slept," and
I simply nod.
"She's a special girl," says Dad.
"I'm...I am..." I struggle for the right words.
"In love?" Dad adds.
"Yes, but something more.
I'm alive when I'm with her.
I can feel my blood flowing.
It might sound strange, but I..."
"You don't need to explain," says Dad.

Then he looks at the picture of Mom again and
Weeps.

Peter comes out from his room,
Enters the living room from the hallway,
Comes up to us both,
Shakes his head.
"I keep telling you that Mom is okay." He turns
And goes back to bed.
"I'll ask her if she's ready yet."
"Wait," I say. "Ready for what?"
"To talk to you both."
Dad and I look at each other, wondering
How seriously we should take Peter's
Conversations with Mom.
He made Audrey a believer,
Perhaps we better believe too.

THIRTY-FIVE

TJ picks us up at my house
For school.
Audrey and I stand
Beside each other,
Sleeping most of Sunday,
Exhausted still.
TJ has energy,
Alone on prom night,
In bed by eleven.

As we enter the school,
A wave of tired upperclassmen file in late,
Filling the hallways in droves.
The dean recording, or trying to
Record, who is tardy.
The school is losing control
Of seniors
That no longer care
To be in their concrete institution,
Which often feels generic,
Prison-like.
I want to skip again.
Go back to our secret spot
By the creek
And have Audrey hold me
While I hold her.

Instead, we drift through
The sea of sleepless bodies.

It's hard to let her go
To class that's on the other side
Of the building.
All I care about is being next to her.
But Audrey said the week prior,
"Let's try to finish the year strong."
She is most likely right
To leave ourselves opportunities,
But I have little.
My grades average,
My ACT score average,
I'm average,
Competing against
Others that aren't.
That's what high school has become,
A competition for colleges,
For your place in society,
One that is made up for you
Before you even graduate.
I don't care to conform.
I want to be like Bruce Springsteen
And be "Born To Run."

On my way to first hour
And another boring class,
Confusing and lost in physics,
Fumbling my way to try to find

A passing grade.
Then something comes my way
Just before I enter the classroom.
Kelsey Richards approaches me
And says, "You know, you've become quite a cutie."
I am taken aback.
She abruptly continues, "You want to do something
    sometime?"
I look around, wondering, not trusting why she's
    suddenly
Talking to me,
The most popular girl in school.
The most fake too.
I answer, "No, I'm good."
It's all I can think of and should be enough.
She doesn't accept that and
Hands me a folded piece of paper,
Her number.
"I'd text you, but no one has your number," she says.
I put the number in my pocket and go into class.
I look back and she's laughing with her
Groupies in the hallway.
Confused,
Somewhat angry,
Why me?

I daydream through the first and second hour,
Pretending to listen, pretending to take notes,
When all I'm thinking about is Audrey and
Our night together.

How gentle she was with me,
Something I never knew I could feel
Since I still struggle even seeing myself naked.
My body,
Violated and ugly,
Taken away from me so many years ago.
Rape made me unsure
Of my own flesh.
I avoid it at all costs.
Foggy mirrors in the bathroom
Are welcome sights.

Audrey doesn't show at lunch.
I wait.
TJ throws his cloth bag on the table.
"What's up?" he says.
"Have you seen Audrey?"
"No," TJ replies, "not since I went to class."
I push my sandwich aside.
Kelsey Richards walks by and waves,
Giggling with her friends.
Why?
She's dating Aaron Anderson,
Crazy athletic football player,
College-bound,
Handsome,
Confident.
Why?
I don't want to get pummeled.
"Dude, what's up with Kelsey giving you the eye?"

TJ says with his mouth full
Of turkey, bread, and mayo.
"You better watch out for Aaron.
He's a beast."
"I don't give a fuck about either of them," I say.
I look around again for Audrey.
Nothing.
Concerned,
I leave.

I go to Student Services and look around.
The woman at the desk asks, "Can I help you?"
I shake my head
And start to leave, then turn.
"Actually, is Audrey down here?"
Nothing.

I head back into the hallways
Where kids eat their lunch,
The ones that have no friends,
The ones that feel like they don't belong,
Sitting against cold, cement walls,
Avoiding eye contact, trying to be invisible.

I walk the hallways, looking in rooms,
Getting frantic,
Worried something happened.
I text her,
Nothing.

Did she try again
To kill herself?
My breathing increases,
I'm starting to spin,
And then I hear Peter
In his classroom
Talking to someone
With a mouthful of peanut butter filling
Between white bread.
It's Audrey!
I enter,
She stares back.
Nothing.

Peter says, "I found her."
I sit at the table.
"What does that mean?"
"I found her in the hallway," he says,
"Crying, so I brought her with me and
Now she's better."
Peter pats Audrey's hand
And then leaves to wash his
Face and hands from
Peanut butter and Cheetos.
"What's going on?" I ask,
Freaking out,
Breath still going crazy,
Leaving my lungs
Faster than I can put it back in.
Audrey is quiet when she speaks.

"Some asshole named Aaron came up and
Gave me
His number and said
He heard I was loose
And wanted to take me out.
So I told him to go fuck himself,
And then he called me a slut and said
I try to ruin
Guys by being a whore."
My face turns calm,
Extremely calm,
Which is what happens when I get that way,
A way I try to avoid.
It's when I want to smash things,
Destroy the world.
"Did he hurt you?" I ask.
She shakes her head. "No, he just
Followed me for a minute, with his stupid friends
Calling me a slut and laughing."
She starts crying again but seems angry more than
Anything and adds,
"It just made me feel dirty again,
And then Peter found me and made me come with him.
Your brother is a healer."
We both smile at that.
"So, Aaron's girlfriend, Kelsey, came to me
And asked me out and gave me her number."
Audrey sits back and then says,
"There are just some people
That can't let others be happy.

They don't want to see people do well,
Probably because they secretly
Can't stand each other."
I'm unsure what to do next.
I could defend my girlfriend's honor,
Be valiant, like in the movies,
And most likely get my ass kicked.
I don't know my next move and become more silent.
"I don't care about either of them," says Audrey,
"I just care about you and what you think of me, but..."
She pauses and looks down at the tile floor,
Cheeto crumbs everywhere.
"He made me feel filthy again,
Like I did before.
As if I did something wrong
For being raped.
I just started to feel good again.
You did that, and in one incident,
I want to wash my skin
Off my body."

I hate the world.
I hate cruelty
And meanness.
Above all,
I hate that she is sad,
Feeling dirty
For something
That someone did to her.
Taking so much from her,

And I know because
I still feel the same.

"I'm just worried that you will..."
I can't say the words, so
Audrey finishes for me.
"Try to kill myself," she says.
"Yeah." I look into her green eyes,
Wanting to be absorbed.
"I told you," she says,
"That I would never do that again,
Never leave you,
I promised..."
She leans over the table and takes my hand.
"And I'll keep my promise."

We walk out into the hall
Hand in hand,
Showing our strength
Together.
Defying odds
And fake people
Doing fake things.
Trying to ruin something
They can't have
In their artificial worlds.
We hold our heads high
And tighten our grips.

THIRTY-SIX

Mr. Johnson looks tired,
Drained and weary.
Something about his eyes
Are dark.
I've seen him this way before,
But today
It is something more.
A cloud seems to follow him,
Engulfed in gray,
Head low.

He gives us all the same greeting
And starts class with a poem,
But doesn't tell us who it is by.
Intentional?
He starts,
"I'm drowning
In judgment
From myself,
The worse critic
My mind
And body
Can have,
Entrapped by
Darkness,
Searching for light.

I need a candle
To light my way
And show me truth."

We all write in silence the entire period,
But I can't write at all,
Steaming from Audrey's interaction
With Aaron and my desire to
Avenge her,
Hurt him.
I want to
Take away her pain through his.
And then there is Mr. Johnson.
I worry looking at him
Stare at his desk,
Struggling in thought,
Maybe not obvious to everyone,
But to me it looks familiar,
That kind of dark stare.
He appears
Numb.
Feeling numb
Is the worst part
Of depression
That no one
Seems to talk about.

Mr. Johnson ends class with some
Words of advice.
Most of us are seniors

And only a few weeks from leaving the
Confines of the public school system
That has benefited some and ruined others,
Depending on
Their beliefs,
Their goals,
Their skin color,
Their religion,
Their empathy as humans,
Because empaths seem to suffer
More around those that aren't.
Mr. Johnson sits on the edge
Of a steel desk, cold and gray.
His tone is darker today.
"I want to share some advice,
Guidance, if you will,
As you move forward in your
Young lives,
Trying to figure it all out."
He pauses and looks around, and then
Mr. Johnson's eyes
Find mine and he continues,
"Live this life by
Your own terms.
Don't let anyone
Influence you to do something that
You don't want to do.
Find your passion,
Your dreams, and go for it.
Even if you think

That dream is far-fetched or
What some may think as foolish.
It's your dream.
Our dreams are what make life
Worth living,
So never stop, even if you
Find yourself ninety and on your
Deathbed,
Never stop going after that
Which you desire.
It's better to die
With your dreams
Still in view than to
Die with never dreaming at all."
The bell rings,
Students don't move.
Silence.
Heads churning,
Mine is spinning.
Glancing at Audrey,
My dream is hers,
To grow old and visit
Waterfalls.

Books are packed.
Young, hopefully inspired
Minds filter out the door,
Still silent.
Some looking back
At Mr. Johnson,

Most likely
Hoping he's right.
Giving them hope
To continue dreaming
No matter what.

Audrey and I
Approach Mr. Johnson,
Who still appears to be lost
In thought,
His back to us with
No class coming in.
When I stand
Directly behind him,
I say, "Mr. Johnson, are you okay?"
He turns, eyes red,
Dark circles following
A route from one side of
His face to the other.
I know that darkness.
Insomnia.
"Oh, hey guys, I'm good."
"Are you?" asks Audrey gently.
His hands go to his eyes.
Mr. Johnson cannot stop from
Releasing his pain.
"I woke up in a pretty dark place,
Depression,
And it's just getting
The better of me today."

I nod, knowing how depression
Can steal away your smile,
Energy,
And leave you feeling
Numb.
Feeling nothing.
"I'll be okay," he says,
"I just need some time to work it out,
Fight the demons." He smiles.
We both step in and hug him.
He's our teacher,
The one who cares,
And I say, "We're here for you too."
He smiles again and says, "I know.
Don't think I don't."
Audrey tells him, "You were there for me
At the hospital, and
I'm here for you.
You're not alone."
Mr. Johnson fist-bumps Audrey,
And then they turn
It into their secret handshake,
With high fives, flipping
Hands, and knuckles again.
"My wife will help me put the
Pieces together later.
She always does.
She's my rock."

I believe someone would
Wonder
Why Mr. Johnson has
Depression.
His life seems so great.
Happily married,
Loves teaching,
Passion for kids.
He's published three books of poems,
So why would he have depression?
It's simple.
Depression doesn't discriminate.
It wants to ruin you,
Ruin everything
Good in your life,
Make you numb to all that
Makes you happy.
Depression is a sneaky
Son of a bitch
And comes at you at all times of the day.
For me, it likes to come at 2:00am
And wake me up to a full head
Of doubt and intrusive thoughts,
Telling me I'm no good
And that everyone will be better off
Without me.
And without knowing it,
I say all of that aloud
While Mr. Johnson and Audrey look on,
Nodding their heads in agreement.

We are the walking wounded,
The thinkers,
Who feel the world
In a different way,
Deeply.
Often misunderstood,
Struggling to hold on
To hope,
But we must
Find a way
To survive.

We walk Mr. Johnson
To the front doors and
Wish him well
As he leaves the building early
To go home,
See his wife,
His rock.

Audrey and I go to Student Services
To ask for a pass
So we aren't marked tardy.
The woman at the desk obliges
As she saw us walking
Mr. Johnson out.
She knew, somehow,
That we were helping,
Not worth a tardy
Or not getting let into class

From some stupid rule.
If a student is more than
Ten minutes late,
They are absent.
Who would go then?

I walk Audrey to class.
He's approaching,
Aaron,
The jock,
The athlete,
The harasser.
I feel Audrey stiffen.
Fear of controlling boys
Still lingers.
That fear
Will always be there.
Her pain,
Unfair
For her to have to
Navigate that pain
For a lifetime.

Aaron passes,
Blows a kiss
To Audrey.
I go blurry,
A whirlwind.
I am
On him,

Punching him
As hard as humanly possible,
As hard as Dylan possible.
I am bringing blood to his face
From his nose,
His mouth,
And I can't stop.
All I see is
White surrounding me
And my target,
His face.

Screaming,
Pulling,
Yanking,
Handcuffs,
Taken.

I find myself in the
Dean's office,
Sitting calmly,
Too calmly,
Not caring
About the consequences.
Waiting with the cop,
Who is talking,
But I'm not listening,
Thinking about where
Audrey is and if
She's safe.

The dean walks in,
Pants still too tight,
Creepy.
Hair must have gotten messed
When he got called to the fight.
I chuckle
Because I've seen him
Try to break up
Fights,
And he looks like
A puppy
Getting swatted for shitting
On the carpet.

They question me,
The cop and dean,
And I feel proven guilty
Before innocent
Until the dean says,
"Audrey told us about Aaron
And what he said this morning
And how he provoked her,
Provoked
You, and that's why
You jumped him."
I nod. "Is she okay?"
"She's fine," says the dean,
Then adds, "Aaron's not."
The cop adds,
"The nurse thinks his

Nose is broken.
They are taking him to the
Emergency room."
They both look at me
For a reaction and get
Nothing,
Because Aaron got what
He deserved.

The cop issues a ticket
And a court appearance
For battery.
The dean gives me
Three days out
Of school.
As if I care.
The ticket bites,
Wasted money,
But being away from assholes
Doesn't bother me.

Dad shows at the door.
The dean invites him in.
He listens to the details
From the cop and dean,
The cop saying, "Dylan didn't
Stop when I came to break it up."
I chime in, "I couldn't hear you,
I was in the middle of a fight."
"Well, you need to stop when

I give commands."
"I'm not a trained dog."
"Dylan," Dad says sternly
And then shakes his head.
"Listen." He clears his throat.
"I'm not condoning fighting, but
I spoke to Audrey before I came
In here, and it sounds like this kid,
Aaron, had it coming."
"No one deserves to get punched,"
Says the dean and then looks at his shiny,
Pointy shoes after
Dad gives him a look that
would burn through steel.
"Again, I don't agree with fighting,
But you must know Audrey's background
and why she came to this school, and this kid
Triggered enough emotion in her
That maybe she should have broken
His nose..."
The dean interrupts again, "And..."
"Stop!" Dad leans in, and for a moment
I picture the dean flying across the room.
"Did you also know that this kid's, Aaron's, girlfriend
Was trying to start some shit by flirting
With my son? They were basically setting
up a scene to break Dylan and Audrey up,
And then the boy called Audrey a whore,
So don't defend this kid like he's an angel.
We're done here," says Dad. "Dylan will

Be back after his suspension,
And he will work off the ticket,
But don't hold this against him because
He is graduating soon and will be done."

Audrey is waiting,
TJ is waiting,
And both give me a hug.
TJ whispers, "You fucked him up."
Dad says, "TJ, not now."
TJ's head goes down. "Sorry."
Audrey takes my hand and
Walks me out to the door.
Dad is on his cell,
Then when he hangs up,
Says, "Audrey, you can come too.
Your dad is calling you out."
Peter is waiting by the front doors
Next to his teacher,
Ready to go.
Backpack on,
He hugs me too,
Not knowing the details,
But Peter can see emotion.
He can feel it.

We walk out together,
Dad and Peter on one side,
Audrey on the other,
TJ trailing behind.

My family,
Protectors,
Surrounding me.

THIRTY-SEVEN

Three days home.
I'm not sure how this is
A punishment.
The dean said
I could come back
Early if I have a
Restorative conference with Aaron.
My reply, "Restore what?
If he harasses my
Girlfriend again,
I'll do the same."
That was the end of the
Conversation.

I am alone, which I don't mind
Except for being away from Audrey,
Who is trying to finish strong
And get the grades that she needs
For college, something she wants to
Do now.
I'm happy for her, but college
Is not in my future,
So I worry
She will leave me.
What will happen?
It seems like we just
Found each other.

I dig some socks out of my drawer,
A pile of white cotton,
And on the bottom,
Weed that has not been smoked
In a long while, sitting there
In a baggy, not needed because
My high is
Her eyes,
Her hair,
Her touch,
Her smile,
Her love,
Her being near.
Still, for some reason
I take it to our backyard
And light up
One last time,
Inhaling something that
Helped me through many
Panic attacks and lonely,
Grieving nights.
It's like saying goodbye
To an old friend
That needs to move on.

Stoned and listening to
Bon Iver,
I start to think of Mom
And all the time we spent
Together

In the backyard,
Playing,
Talking,
Breathing,
Practicing yoga,
And I cry.
I cry
Stoned tears,
Frightened because
Those times are over.
I practice breathing
As my mind has had
Too much time
To wonder,
And even inhaling
Deep isn't helping.
Intrusive thoughts enter
That Audrey had helped capture
And make dormant,
But being alone,
They are free to roam,
To run and fly.

I leave the warmth of
May air for the inside of
The house and go directly to
The photo album next to Dad's chair,
Where he leaves it to remember
All the good times,
Their youth,

What he's lost.
And as I start the
Journey
With Mom in high school
And Dad next to her,
Doing what we now call a "selfie"
With old-school cameras,
I'm taken aback because
It's not that photo album.
Instead,
It's Mom pregnant with Peter,
Laughing, glowing with her
First child, already empowering him
To be his best.
And then the next page,
Me inside her belly
That Dad thought funny
To draw a smiley face on.
She looks tired but ready,
And then there she is,
Lined up for a marathon she
Was running,
So able and strong,
Full of life.
And our vacation to Canada,
Hiking and camping,
Trying to avoid bears in a
Place called Banff,
A trip where I fell in love
With the mountains surrounding me,

Feeling alive,
Ten years old.
Then it's there,
Slapping me in the face.
New Mexico
At twelve.
Our arrival,
Still smiling,
The last picture
On the page, and
I fear,
Turning the glossy photos
To see what's next.
I pause,
I grip the sides,
Breathe faster
In anticipation
Of memory.
Uncle Kipp's arm around me,
With Grandma and Grandpa
Still smiling,
Just before my smile
Disappeared.
I struggle for a moment
As I see me leaning into Kipp.
Did I cause this?
The thought increases,
My heart rate
Pounding,
To think it was me

Somehow telling him it was okay.
I stop, slam the album shut,
Slap my face as if to snap me out
Of this fixated thought that
Somehow
I caused my own rape,
And I scream out,
Tears falling to cleanse me,
My voice loud, "Fuck you! I was
Only a little kid.
Fuck you!
I was
So happy...so fuck..."
I am unsure again who I
Am screaming at,
Me or Kipp.
As I calm,
I go back to the pictures,
Curious to see my
Young eyes,
Youthful smile,
Which had all but darkened and
Disappeared
After the rape,
After Kipp took away
My childhood.

As I keep my journey going,
I see a kid that tried to hang on
Through middle school.

My hair grew long, my face hardened.
It was a time when I was arrested twice,
Once for shoplifting shoes
And punching the manager who tried
To stop me,
Another for stealing a car with its engine
Running in front of a store
In the dead of winter. People
Often did that to keep warm,
So I timed it right and took off,
Crashing three miles
Away into a snowbank.
More pictures.
Freshman year,
Back in Banff.
Mom and Dad thought
Mountain air
Would help their suddenly
Delinquent
Kid who was going off the
Deep end.
Getting suspended three times
By the dean, a different one,
Until one morning, early,
I snuck from the tent,
Walked up the trailhead
To a cliff, and leaned into it.
I felt like I was flying,
With cool air hitting my face,
Ready for takeoff.

I stepped closer
To the edge.
Death was near.
Pain would be gone
Within moments.
Just one more step and
It would be over.

Mom pulled me back.
Me
Landing on
Her.
She held me tight, rubbing my hair.
We both cried as she said,
"What happened to you?
What happened to my Dylan,
My smiling boy?"
And it was my chance to
Confess.
Instead, my voice was
Dead,
Silent.
I didn't want to make Mom cry
Anymore, so I stopped getting suspended,
Stopped stealing,
And turned to isolating myself from
Everyone but Mom, Dad, Peter, and TJ.
Muddling through sophomore year,
Junior year,
Invisible.

And then, I see the pictures
Just before we found out
That she was sick,
Already looking tired,
But her eyes fierce,
Preparing for what was to come,
A war, a battle
That she would lose.
My photo journey ends,
And I close the book of
Memories.

Memories can be
Like a knife to
The brain,
Puncturing the good parts,
Waking up the bad.

I must have fallen asleep,
Wanting to forget
My waking nightmare.
I wake up to a knocking door.
I look at my phone.
It is 12:30pm.
There are three texts from Audrey.
"Are you up?"
"Hey, call me."
"Okay, I'm worried.
Coming over."
Another knock,

A little louder.
I shake the sleep from my head
And scramble for the door.
Beautiful Audrey,
Standing before me,
Coming into me,
Embrace.

"Hey, I was worried.
Why didn't you answer?"
"I'm sorry, I fell asleep."
"Yeah, I can see that." She laughs
From the struggle that
Her fingers are having to move
Through my tangled hair.
"Are you doing okay?" she asks.
She knows. We have come
To know one another well,
Well enough to know when the other
Is struggling. "You have eyes," she says, then adds,
"Old ghost?"
I nod and try to
Hold tears back because
Sometimes it feels
Like too many have been shed.
"Too much time to think.
No distractions, so, you know,
Monkey mind," I say.
We laugh because we both know exactly
What that feels like.

Monkey mind
Never stops moving,
Screaming,
Throwing shit.

Audrey comes in, lunch in hand.
"I brought you a sandwich."
We sit, eating in silence because
My mind goes immediately
To my photo journey through the album of
Memories
That proves I was once happy and when,
Exactly when,
Everything
Was taken from me.
"Dylan." Audrey releases my thoughts as
I feel her hand on mine.
"Tell me what's going on." She leans in and
Softly kisses me.
"And I'll give you another one of those."
Her smile warms me
And makes me want to tell her everything.
I go and get the photo album and bring it back
To the kitchen table, where I start to open
Each page, one by one,
Explaining my history,
Showing her when I was innocent,
Clean.
I stop at a picture.
Audrey sees my face,

Calm and pure.
I show her Uncle Kipp and nod.
No words.
She knows, her face turning
To part anger, part fear,
Part sorrow.
And then after,
She knows because
My eyes have changed
In the photos.
Pain always comes through the eyes,
Hopelessness leaves through them,
And she sees a boy, as the pages flip,
Who is suffocating
Like she is
Through a memory that he wishes could be
Erased,
Deleted.
And then Mom, who suffers
So young and ages so fast,
With chemicals attacking her soul.
And as the last page closes,
Audrey sighs and leans in, holding me.
"They are just memories," she says.
"I'm here now, right here, holding you,
And you're holding me, and maybe that's enough."
New memories might be enough.

Hope
Sometimes is enough

To weather the storm
In your mind,
And it seizes
Your hands
From hurting you
Because living
Now has meaning,
Purpose.

"I'm staying with you." Audrey sits up.
"I don't want you getting in trouble," I say,
"The dean is already watching us."
Audrey holds my face softly and says,
"When have I ever said something
Without following through? I'm not worried
About it. They can call my parents, and I'll
Tell them exactly where I was and why. They'll
Understand."

I keep falling in love with her more
Every day.
I'm still not sure how love works,
Though it seems to be working
Well.
It's a mystery,
One I don't want to solve
Since she says she loves me back
Every day,
And that is solution enough
To live a life,
One that's

Mindful,
Like Prudence
Advises.

We leave the house for the path
To the oak tree
And stop to hug our tree.
Then to the creek
Where we last made love
And replicate it all
Over again.
The water races
From the previous day's rain,
And then we lie back,
Her head on my chest,
Looking at the treetops sway
And the sun move a little further
Into the afternoon.
Sometimes the best moments
Are in silence,
Where you simply feel
The other person's
Presence within you,
Listening and feeling
Each other's breath
Until your breathing
Becomes one.
Solace,
Security,
Hope.

THIRTY-EIGHT

That evening, I ask Audrey to go to yoga.
Dad and Peter have been practicing at home.
Dad has it in his head that he wants to become
Better before going back to a class.
I tell him that's not what yoga is about,
A competition.
It's really just you and your mat,
Moving your body,
Calming your mind.
Peter has mastered Savasana,
The only person I've ever known
To do so because Savasana
Is the toughest pose.
Usually intrusive thoughts
Enter when still.
Audrey agrees to go.
I tell her about Prudence
And how she's become therapy
For my dark mind.

Audrey borrows a mat from the studio.
We are greeted by Prudence before
Going into the hot room.
"A guest?"
I nod.
"This is Audrey," I say.

They shake hands.
"Nice to meet you," says Audrey,
"I've heard so much about you."
"Thank you, and
Dylan's a very sweet boy." Prudence
Motions for us to enter.

Our mats are next to each other
As we lie there
In silence,
Simply breathing and listening
To a playlist,
One I made for Prudence.
Audrey is smiling as she knows
Each song, every word
Because she has heard them over and over,
My standby songs for lonely nights
And drifting days.
Gregory Alan Isakov,
Nick Drake,
Iron & Wine,
Damien Rice,
Bon Iver,
Ben Howard,
Alexi Murdoch,
Glen Hansard,
John Lennon,
Simon & Garfunkel.
They have all talked to me at some point
In the loneliest of places,

And now they speak to Audrey
And Prudence.

The class begins.
Admittedly
Struggling to focus
With Audrey so close,
My mind drifts toward her
With each movement,
Each flow
And breath,
And at the end
On our backs,
I reach for her hand.
Her touch sweaty,
Not unlike the creek,
And I absorb all of her.
Prudence continues
Savasana longer than usual
As she sits at the edge
Of her mat, breathing.
I drift and sleep,
If only for a moment,
And wake up
Disoriented, looking for
Mom.
My heart falls in sorrow
When reality slaps me in the face
That she still isn't there.
Sleep can fool you,

Or maybe being awake can.
Especially since most of us
Walk around asleep,
Unaware,
In our daily lives.

Prudence is next to me,
Speaking softly with Audrey.
She sees my fear,
They both do,
And I struggle to clear
My head.
And at once,
Audrey takes my left hand,
Prudence my right.
A woman's touch
On both sides,
Strength,
Security,
And a gentleness
That is needed
In this world.

"It's common," Prudence says softly,
"To fall asleep in Savasana.
It's good for you
And tells me that you are
Deeply relaxed." She's
Speaking more to Audrey than to me.
"Becoming that relaxed, which we humans

Often cannot, brings us to
A deep place of emotion."
There is grace in Prudence's voice,
And it immediately calms me,
A healer and whisperer to all
Who are damaged.
Audrey's face is calm,
Calmer than I have seen it,
Reflecting from the soft
Glow of light
And electric candles.

"I have some time, and the studio is free," says
Prudence.
I adjust my position and am seated upright,
Legs crossed, and I reach for Audrey's hand.
It's become so familiar.
Prudence smiles at the gesture.
"How are you both doing?" she asks.
Audrey looks at me, and I can't
Take my eyes off of her.
I'm beaming.
"Honestly..." My comfort level with Prudence
Is similar to my Mom because she is like
My second mom.
I call her my "Yoga Mom," which she loves.
"Audrey is the best thing that's happened to me," I say
Without hesitation or caring if it sounds corny
Or cliché.
Audrey feels my sincerity and naturally leans into me,

Shoulder to shoulder.

"I can see, actually feel, that you love each other," Prudence

Says, "I believe you already have something rare,

Worth hanging on to with all your might,

Which might prepare you for

A life together."

"Prepare?" Audrey asks curiously.

"You will be challenged. You already have. I know

Dylan has, and he has shared some of your story

With me." I suddenly worry that Audrey will be

Angry that I told Prudence

About her assault,

But she smiles instead.

"You are going to have people doubt your love

Simply because of your age.

There will be some that will not want to see you

Happy,

Having something they don't, and they will try to

Ruin it."

Audrey and I look at each other and

Nod because it's something

That has already happened.

Prudence continues, "Of course, life itself can bring

Suffering,

As you already know.

It's part of life, something we can't avoid.

However, it's how you handle the suffering,

What you do with it, that will matter."

Prudence, I know, has suffered

Like many of us, and I have heard

This lesson before, but hearing it with
My love
Brings a different, new meaning to it.

"Audrey, I see so much strength in you."
Prudence takes
Audrey's hand and massages it.
"You have someone in Dylan
Who loves you, and that often is enough."
"I love him," Audrey says directly to Prudence
Like she forgot I was here for a moment.
"He's saved me from myself, from my..."
Then Audrey breaks, which can happen after yoga and
Talking with Prudence
Because being vulnerable is what Prudence
Brings to you.
Prudence continues to massage Audrey's hand
And then takes mine as we all
Sit in a modified triangle.
Sweaty hands,
Breathing in, there is
Calm in our collective strength.

On our walk home,
We decide to stop at Bridges.
Tea in hand,
Sitting by a foggy window
On a cool May night,
Our silence breaks.
"Prudence is amazing," says Audrey,

274

"It's so calming just being near her,
As if she's figured the world out
And how to protect herself from it."
I agree with a nod. "She has her own story."
Audrey swirls her tea bag.
"I'm sure if you continue to go
See her with me, she will tell you."
"To be that calm, she must have
Suffered like she talks about,
And maybe figured out how
To suffer better.
Does that make any sense?"
Audrey chuckles to herself, but she always
Makes sense to me.
I affirm that it makes total sense.
"She has depression, caused by
Childhood trauma,
An abusive mother.
She was the only child
And took her mom's wrath
Until they removed her
From the home."
"Oh my God," Audrey says.
"I feel so bad for her, but to see her
So calm and knowing the world like she does,
She's amazing. It's...hopeful."
"She is," I agree, "and I'm glad I finally
Introduced you to her. She is special in my life."
"But how does she know so much about love?
Is she married?"

"She is. She met her partner, Theresa, when she was
Traveling through Europe in her early thirties."
"That's amazing." Audrey leans in closer.
"They met on a train and then got off in some small
Village in Portugal and went to a café to talk,
And then just kept traveling
With each other, and the rest is history.
Theresa comes into the studio
Every once in a while and takes a class."

Audrey says, "We should do that."
"What?"
"Travel Europe when we graduate."
We have told each other how much we love
The other
And have spoken about our feelings
Here, in the moment, but to mention
A future together,
After high school,
Sends goosebumps up my arm.
"Well..." Audrey pauses.
"That's, if you want to?"
"Yeah," I speak up what feels
Eager, but I needed to get it out,
To confirm my love and
Willingness
To spend a life with her.
Audrey giggles.

"Where would we go first?"
"To Bled, Slovenia." Audrey doesn't
Hesitate with her response.
"So, you've thought about this?" I take her hand.
"Yup." She pulls up pictures on her phone
And shows me. "We can take a boat ride to the
Island in the middle of the lake." She points to
The picture of the island. A church is there.
Audrey continues, "We can go to this church and ring
    the bell.
Rumor has it, all your dreams will come true."
I lean in for a soft kiss, loving her excitement
And hopeful curiosity, and whisper,
"What if they already have?"

We walk home.
She holds my arm
Just above the elbow,
And I wonder for a moment
If our dreams are just
Thoughts that will never play out.
Or are they real?
I hope
That we will stand in the
Island church,
In a place I have
Never heard of,
Ringing a bell that
Makes dreams come true.

As we walk,
A car pulls up.
Aaron comes out
With three friends.
I'm down on
The ground,
They are on top.
I'm feeling trapped,
A feeling I've had before,
Helpless
In my body
And mind,
And they don't stop
Punching me,
Kicking me.
I try to move,
But I'm restrained.
I look at Audrey,
Trying to plead
For her to run,
But Aaron grabs her
Just as I black out.

THIRTY-NINE

I wake up in a strange room.
The light shines above me.
I'm confused,
Wondering why I'm lying down,
Pain in my head,
In my stomach,
All over.
I look over, feeling
Someone near me.
"Peter," I whisper.
He smiles.
He has my hand
In his,
Rubbing it softly.
It's wrapped up,
Bandaged.
"Mom told me not to leave you," says Peter.
Stillness.

Suddenly, I rise up, and
It becomes clear
Why I'm here, in a hospital.
"Audrey," I say loudly,
"Audrey!"
Peter hugs me,
Not wanting me to move,
His strength,

Physical and mental,
Is beyond mine.
I yell her name again, "Audrey!"
The nurse comes in,
And then Dad.
I'm squeezed between
Dad and Peter.
My ribs hurt,
But I don't care,
Lacking air, I gasp, "Audrey?"
In Dad's ear.
"She's doing okay," he says.
And I cry
At the image of her face,
Frightened as Aaron takes hold
Of her,
My last memory.

"She's a couple of rooms down, Dylan," says Dad.
"Is she...okay?"
"Yes, just bruised up and in shock, but
They said she will be fine."
"Did they rape her?"
It's my first thought and I need to know
As my mind and the room are spinning,
Waiting for an answer
That seems garbled coming from
Dad's mouth as the
Adrenaline plugs my ears
And blurs my eyes.

"No." Dad is shaking his head too.
I need the nonverbal.
"That boy had hold of her wrist, and she
Fought so hard that her right wrist is broken
And her lip is swollen from biting his arm."
Dad smiles at that.
"She's strong, Dylan.
A lot of fight in her.
Reminds me of your mom."
Peter chimes in, "And Mom says for me to help you."
"I want to see her," I say,
"I need to see that she's okay."
"Soon enough," says Dad.
"Her mom and dad and Mr. Johnson are with her."
"Mr. Johnson?"
"Yeah," Dad says, nodding,
"He was the one that chased the boys off.
He happened to be driving by, pulled up, and
Threw two kids off you.
I'm talking airborne." Dad laughs at that.
"Audrey said he called 911
Because you were knocked out, and
The boys fled in their car.
Little fuckers."

Peter is still stroking my hand and
Holding it against his face.
Dad goes to check on Audrey
Since I can't go down there yet.

I lie back on the pillow, trying to recall
Everything.
It happened so quick, but most
Traumatic events do.
I remember the boys on me,
Holding me down,
Restrained,
And that sick,
Claustrophobic feeling
Surging through me,
Helpless.
I haven't felt like that since
Uncle Kipp
Held me down.
Lying on me.
Raping me.
I cry.
Peter leans in.
"Mom says you will be okay."
I don't cry for me,
I cry for Audrey
Because she had to have
Those same thoughts
As Aaron grabbed her,
Violating her freedom to move.

Mr. Johnson comes through the glass door.
He looks tired,
Drained.
"Dylan." He stands next to Peter,

Hand on Peter's shoulder.

"I wish I could have gotten there earlier," he says.

"It sounds like you came just in time," I reassure him.

"Well, I'm not sure how far they would have gone."

"I heard you made them fly," I say, smiling.

"I guess." Mr. Johnson grins, then adds,

"I'm probably going to have to answer to the principal
And the school board why I was tossing some kids
    around."

"Fuck that," I say.

Peter looks up and stops rubbing my hand. "Don't swear."

"You were just helping us. You saved us," I demand.

"Yeah, they'll still question it. Teachers are always
    under the
Microscope," Mr. Johnson says.

He is right.

"They better not do anything or
We will all be at school
Telling them what's up.
There will be protests if they try to
Remove you."

Mr. Johnson smiles. "I appreciate that, but you just rest.
I think they're letting you go soon.
You've got a cracked rib and bruises.
You can take a beating."

He gives a light push with
His fist against my arm.

I can take a beating.

I can take it all.

Mr. Johnson says goodbye
And leaves the hospital.
Peter looks at me. "I'm your bodyguard."
"Yes, Peter. You are."
He grins with pride.

Dad is back,
Audrey next to him,
Her parents behind.
She comes in
On the opposite side of Peter
And leans over.
Her hair softly covering me,
She wraps around me
And kisses me
With meaning
On my cheek.
The best medicine
For my pain,
Her love.

"Peter," says Dad,
"Let's step out for a minute."
Everyone leaves.
The curtain closes,
And we don't say anything
For a moment as we
Take each other in.
This is where I want to be,
In her arms.

"Are you okay?" I ask,
Breaking the silence.
"I am." Audrey raises her head
And continues, "My wrist hurts,
And my lip. I bit that asshole so hard,
And when he jerked away, he hit my lip.
I saw him pulling his fist back,
About to hit me, and then he went
Flying
Into his car.
Mr. Johnson is strong as hell."
We both smile.
"I want to kill those fuckers."
Audrey says "no" with a gesture
As her auburn hair sways.
"My dad already pressed charges.
The cops have them, and the street cam shows
Everything. They're busted."
"Good" is all I say,
Except my face says I want them.
I want all of them to die
For what they did to me,
But mostly what they did to her.
"Dylan, let this go. They aren't worth it."
"Yeah, you're probably right. I just...
I couldn't help you and it's...
Tearing me up."
"How could you? You had three guys on you,
And besides..." She smiles. "I can help myself."
And she's right.

She doesn't need me to fight
Her battles.
She's a warrior in her own right.

"I worry," I say and pause.
"I worry about you being grabbed like that."
"It's just my wrist," she says. "It will heal."
"No, not that," I say. "I'm worried about
What this will do to you,
Being grabbed like that,
If it will bring back memories."
"Well," Audrey starts.
"That will heal too."
And she comes back to me and gently kisses
Me with a swollen lip that feels tender
As we embrace.
"Let's go to that church," I whisper.
She smiles, and I can't take
My eyes off of her.

Our parents enter.
Peter stands by my side again,
My bodyguard.
"They're letting you go soon," says Dad.
"Good! I want out of here."
The doctor comes in.
"We're releasing you,
Just take it slow. Those ribs
Will take a few weeks to heal."
Then he adds, "You're lucky."

I look around the room at the faces
Staring back at me
With love.
"Yes, I am," I reply.

FORTY

My suspension is over.
Back at school.
So is Aaron
And the boys that joined him,
Beating me,
Hurting Audrey.
The principal,
The dean,
Gave my dad a line
That they couldn't be
Punished at school
Because the fight happened
Outside of school.
Fight?
I was attacked.
They received tickets,
Community service.
Audrey and I receive
Harassment,
Bullying
From some kids.
Friends of Aaron,
Snickering,
Social media threats
That it'll happen again.
We also have others.
Kids that come from nowhere

It seems,
Telling us they appreciate
Our strength,
Our resilience.

And other girls
Coming forward,
Speaking to Audrey
About what happened to her,
Her rape,
Saying they believe her,
That they have faced similar.
It's as if Audrey's bruised wrist has become
A bandaged
Badge of courage,
Giving girls the ability to speak up.
Our school,
Divided more than ever.
Popular boys being accused
Of groping girls,
Getting them drunk,
Taking advantage.
Nudes that were shared in private
Found on phones.
Friends of the offenders
Making shirts that say
Stop The Witch Hunt
As if they are condoning
Rape.
Condoning

Sharing nudes of minors.
Girls that falsely and naively
Trusted boys they sought approval from
To never share.
Nothing ever happens to the offenders.
Phones confiscated.
Tickets.
Back in school.
Little accountability.
The victimized feeling embarrassed.
Except this time,
Maybe for once,
They have a growing voice
To help them yell,
"Enough!"

The end of our senior year comes.
Graduation invites are being sent out,
Doctored photos on shiny paper,
Seniors wearing their chosen college
Shirts to represent where they are going,
And I struggle to come up with a shirt
Because college is not my future.
I'm not sure what is,
So I just wear black.
Audrey wears tie-dye,
Though she's been accepted to two colleges,
Florida and an art college in New York City.

I see Aaron and his cronies
Every day in the halls.

They never noticed me before,
But they do now
And they stay away,
Almost looking down,
Ordered to stay clear,
Away from me and Audrey.
And with the other voices around school
Speaking up,
They have been deflated.
Bruised egos
Disappearing as the days of May
March to an end.

I never thought I would want high school to continue.
I've been waiting for four years to get away,
Out of these cold walls,
Walls that have betrayed me
Until I met her,
My strength,
And now that it's here,
The end,
I wonder where it went.
Perhaps I'm longing for
Missed opportunities
That never came,
Or it's because this is where I
Found Audrey again
After so many years.
The fear of losing her swells.

FORTY-ONE

We walk to the path,
The field,
And surround the oak tree
With our arms,
Then venture to the creek,
A quiet trickle.
The lack of rain
Leaves little current.
It's as if time slowed
But still changed.

"I want you to come with me," says Audrey
As we lean against the log next to the creek.
"I don't know what I would do in a big city," I say.
"Be with me," she says.
"Of course," I say, "but...I'm not sure if I should leave."
"It's not like a regular college. I won't be going to keggers,
Football games, and acting like, well,
I don't know what college students act like."
"I just don't know if I should leave Dad and Peter.
It's still less than a year since
My mom died, and
Dad might need me."
Silence, except the shallow water
And wind blowing the treetops.
Audrey's eyes change,
A little less light, less green, if possible.

"I'm afraid," she says.
"I am too," I agree.
"If you don't come with me,
We may lose each other for good."
She leans into me.
I want to beg her to stay.
I think about putting a guilt trip on her,
Forcing her to reconsider,
Telling her I may not make it
Without her.
I can't do it.
I know it's something she wants,
A way to get away, live her dreams,
Get her degree at some fashion institute,
And if she wants it, I want it for her
Because that is love.
We lie back in silence,
The green leaves looking down at us,
Waving,
Her head resting on my chest.
My dream.

We have yet to make love indoors.
Only at this safe spot,
Secret spot,
Where thoughts are shared
With the trees
And carried away with the water.
I look at her.
"My world is you." I kiss her softly.

She responds without words,
Only movement
That says everything and nothing
All at once.
"I found you,
I found me,
Somewhere between the trees and clouds,
And I never want to let you go.
You have become my breath, my life,
And my heartbeat, and I need my heart
To keep beating, feeling full and strong,
And..." I pause, roll to face her,
Appreciating that she lets me talk
This way to her, about my love for her.
I realize what I must do.
I simply nod and smile.
It's all she needs, and she smiles at me,
Lying over me again,
Her head on my chest,
Hair tickling my nose,
And whispers,
"Somewhere between the trees and clouds."

FORTY-TWO

Graduation is in one week,
And I now have to break the news to Dad
And Peter that I will be going with Audrey
To a city that I have never been to,
One of the largest in the world,
And try to find my place in it.
Uncertain,
Excited,
A new start,
A new life.
At least a new chapter
Of this life.

I see Prudence first,
My confidant,
My guide,
And sit after class
In the heat,
Relaxed from flowing,
Breathing.
"Audrey asked me to leave with her
To New York. I told her I would go,
But I'm scared. I'm still not sure
I should leave Dad and Peter."
Prudence is silent,
Thinks for a moment before responding,
As she always does.

"You will never be sure," she says.
I'm confused.
Not what I wanted to hear.
I wanted certainty.
"You can never be sure about much
Of anything in life or how it will work out."
Prudence sits straight on her mat.
"Dylan, life is full of moments
Meant for you to capture.
Sometimes they just appear, testing you
And seeing if you will take them
To change your path, your journey.
There will be times when you
Won't even notice
The moment and it will pass,
Leaving you in a stalemate,
Stagnant.
Every so often, something or
Someone will stand before you,
Offering a new direction,
And you need to be aware enough,
Willing to go into the unknown,
The uncertain,
And simply experience life.
Otherwise, you may never truly live."

I leave the yoga studio knowing
What I need to do.
But I want one more conversation,
One more consultation.

Mr. Johnson is at school early
The next morning. I tell Audrey
I will meet her there.
"Hey, everything good?" Mr. Johnson asks,
Immediately thinking something has
Happened to one of his kids.
"Yeah, I just need to talk."
He gestures toward the chair that
Sits next to his desk.
I start right in,
"Audrey is going to a fashion school in
New York City."
He nods. "Yeah, she mentioned that."
"You know?" I'm a little taken aback that
She told a teacher
Before me, but I guess it's Mr. Johnson,
And here I am talking to him
Without telling Audrey.
Double standards.
"She told me when she applied.
I wrote a letter of recommendation,
And she told me when she was accepted."
"Well, she asked me to go with her."
"That's awesome!" says Mr. Johnson,
Already telling me his answer to my question.
"I'm not sure I should go," I say, and then add,
"With my mom dying, I feel like I need to
Stay with my dad and Peter."
"Yeah, I get it," says Mr. Johnson,
"But this is your life, Dylan.

You are the one that
Needs to live it."
"I suppose, but Peter can be
Tough to live with sometimes,
and Dad might need me."
I'm looking for an excuse to stay, or
Maybe just permission to go.
"You have one life to live.
You have a girl that wants you to
Start living that life with her.
Take the chance.
Go for it!
I see you two together, and
I can tell that you are crazy about each other."
"I really want to, but I guess I'm scared.
I have no idea what I'll do."
"Maybe..." Mr. Johnson sits forward,
Leaning toward me.
"Just maybe, all you need to do
Is love her, and
That will be enough."

FORTY-THREE

Floating,
Drifting mindlessly
Through the last week of school,
Unaware of anything but
The thought of
Loving Audrey
For a lifetime,
Starting a life
Together.

The last day comes.
We walk hand in hand
To lunch.
The stares from kids have ended,
The division has ended,
And it seems like
Everything is
Back to normal in school.
Girls taking nudes,
Sending them to boys,
Wanting approval.
Body-shaming,
Harassment,
Assaults.
It seems like
There's no justice,

A never-ending
Cycle.

TJ comes to the table,
A tray of food and a letter.
"I made it," he says and
Hands me an envelope.
"What's this?" I open it.
Stanford!
He got into Stanford University.
TJ, always smart.
TJ, always loyal.
TJ, always there.
"Congrats!" I fist-bump him.
Audrey hugs him.
"That's amazing!" she says.
TJ shrugs. "It's cool, I guess."
"Aren't you excited?" asks Audrey.
"I am," says TJ as he bites into his sandwich,
Mustard landing on the table.
"We're going opposite directions," says Audrey.
"Yeah, you will be far away from us," I add.
TJ stops chewing. "Us?" he asks.
Audrey looks over. "Us?"
I smile at her, and she leans in and hugs me.
Approval.
"Cool," says TJ. "Now I have a place to visit."
"Dude, Stanford. That's huge." I tap the letter.
TJ just keeps chewing.
Audrey and I look at each other,

Wondering.

"Are you okay?" asks Audrey.

"I'm good. My parents can't afford it.

I'm not sure why I even applied.

Probably just to see if I could get in."

Then TJ pulls two other letters from his pocket,

One from Harvard and one from Oxford.

"This...is amazing!" I hold the letters, looking at TJ.

"I'll probably just go to a state college," he says, then chuckles,

"It'll really piss off my counselor if I do.

He helped me get my applications

And letters ready and

Wants to brag about a student

Getting accepted into these schools.

He said it was 'Good for our high school.'

Fuck that. I could care less about this school."

"Well, you should think about a way to go

To one of these schools," I say.

TJ just keeps eating and

Dismisses my comment,

Knowing that there is no way he can

Afford it.

So many times in life,

We are halted from dreams,

Something we long to do

Or should have done,

And regret follows.

I feel as if there are

Thousands
Of gray-haired people
Walking around,
Wounded by regret from
The life they didn't live,
The chances they didn't take.
Regret is the worst sin
Because it means you
Forgot to fulfill your dreams,
Or at least go after them.

We walk up to Mr. Johnson's room,
Our last class with him.
We hold hands through the halls,
Not saying a word.
Audrey with a smile on her face,
The same as mine,
Knowing we will venture into
The unknown, but we will
Be taking the journey together.
Taking chances.
In the stairwell,
Audrey stops,
Pulls me in,
A kiss,
Meaningful,
Intentional,
Loving.

Mr. Johnson is
High-fiving kids in the hall,
Standing in the middle
As they zoom by,
Eager
To leave the school in two more hours.
Seniors screaming,
The school losing control
Because we will be done
With high school
Forever.
The dean,
With his slicked-back hair,
Pointy leather shoes,
Too tight pants,
Trying to be hip,
Can't keep control.
So he leans,
Securing himself
Against the wall,
Attempting to look subtle.
Instead, he
looks frightened.
He escapes down the stairs.

Mr. Johnson comes in,
Looks over the class,
His kids.
"These moments are my best
And my worst," he says.

We listen.
We always listen,
Awaiting to hear what's next
From this man
Who seems to know
Secrets
About the world
That most do not,
Except maybe Mom
And Prudence.
I wonder
For a moment,
One day,
Will I know the
World
Enough for someone to
Listen to me?
"I've gotten to see you
All grow, develop into
Writers through the year
And express yourselves,
Write down your dreams
And make them real,
Bring them
To life."
Mr. Johnson takes a
Step toward us.
"You have either brought your
Characters to life
And given them breath and a

Heartbeat,
Or brought yourselves,
Your personal
Stories,
Ambitions,
Fears,
Desires,
To your writing
And given them the same
Heartbeat.
I applaud you."
He claps for us,
And we cheer back and for
Each other and then
Calm.
And then he starts
What we all anticipate daily,
A reading,
Something with meaning.
A Poem.
One he reads with passion.
When he says,
"Rage, rage against the dying of the light,"
Mr. Johnson has meaning in his voice,
As if he wants us to absorb the words into our skin.

Mr. Johnson gently lays
The book down
On his desk and
Pauses before turning.

"A poem by Dylan Thomas,
'Do Not Go Gentle Into That Good Night.'"
He looks around slowly
To eager eyes and minds.
"Go and live your lives,
Be true to yourself
Always,
And live a life
Worth writing about,
By your own terms,
Your own ambitions.
This journey that we are all on
Takes us on different paths,
Only to come together
When the last bell rings,
And when the day is done,
Have no regrets,
For you gave it your all
And didn't go easy.
Instead, you
'Rage, rage against the dying of the light.'"

The principal,
His name
I forget,
Announces for us,
The seniors,
To gather
In the middle of the
Commons

For a paper toss,
Where we can dispose of
All of our hard work
Or incomplete work
From the year.
What seniors know is that
The tradition has a purpose:
To gather all the junk
Into one pile so it's easier for
The custodians to gather
And fewer headaches for the
Principal and dean.
So much for traditions
Being about students.

I walk out the doors of the school,
TJ on one side of me,
Audrey on the other,
And we walk happily.
TJ turns and flips the school off.
I turn and give it a nod.
Audrey keeps looking straight ahead,
Set on a future that awaits,
No looking back.

TJ drops us off at Audrey's.
The time has come
To end our high school
Journey together,
And we are now on

To something else,
Something unknown
That scares the hell out of me.
Audrey leans in,
Kissing me softly,
And I oblige.
She turns and says,
"Stay gold, Ponyboy."
I think S.E. Hinton
Would love Audrey.

FORTY-FOUR

My legs take me
Past my home
To a path I've walked on
For years.
A thousand times
Alone.
To a field that leads
To a tree that I have
Come to know
Every shape and texture,
And running water
That slows when the rain
Decides to leave.
A place I call my sanctuary.
One I'm not sure,
Not certain
Or brave enough
To leave.

I sit quietly,
Throwing rocks,
Like throwing
My thoughts
Into the creek
To be washed
Away.
A million thoughts

Lie on the bottom
From years of
Contemplation.
Then I stand,
Undress, and walk
Slowly into the creek,
Where cold water steals
My breath.
The rocky bottom
Challenges my balance,
And I feel the
Current rushing
Against my knees.
I look down at my body,
Too skinny,
Too pale.
Even alone
In cold waters
Among the trees,
I am ashamed
Of my naked self.

For a moment, I think of
Falling back,
Hitting my head on stone,
Knocking myself unconscious,
Drifting under,
Losing breath.
It's something I think about
From time to time,

Producing my death.
If I fell back,
No one would know.
They would think it was an
Accident.
Instead, I suddenly
Hug myself,
My skin,
As if to hold me back
Because there seems
To be two voices
Inside my head.
One says
Death.
One says
Life.
An internal tug of
War.
That's depression.

I attempt to shake
The dark thoughts
From my head
And whisper,
"Why would I do that?"
My voice tries to reason with my
Mind,
With the wind
And water.
I have it okay.

I have a girl who loves me,
Wants to spend her life with me,
A father who supports me and does
His best, what fathers should do,
And Peter, who will always be loyal.
TJ, Prudence, Mr. Johnson,
Even Audrey's parents.
I am loved.
Still, Prudence has told me,
"Your depression will sometimes
Test you
And try to take from you
Everything,
And make you think you have
Nothing."

I walk backwards,
Looking down at the rocks
Below my feet,
My fingertips gently
Skimming the top
Of the water.
I see my blurred reflection
And try to smile at my
Foolishness
And then realize
How much I judge my
Own thoughts
That I cannot always
Control.

My smile in the moving water
Turns
To a frown,
And then I smile bigger,
Attempting to look more
Happy,
Playing with the water and
Trying to
Convince my reflection that I am
Happy.
The current turns my face into a
Blurred frown,
Dark.

I move to a shallow spot,
One where I can sit and let the
Water cleanse me and
My body and mind.
I lie back,
Looking at the treetops
Sway in the gentle breeze,
The June air tickling my
Nose and ears, and I'm
Submerged,
Where all sound is
Muffled
Except that of running water,
And for a moment I
Wonder,
Is this what fish hear?

I rise up, suddenly aware
That I do not want to say
Goodbye
To my secret place,
The trees
And creek,
Without Audrey,
Because it is not just my space
Anymore, but
Ours.
I sit by the downed log,
Drying off in the breeze,
Then get dressed.
Two texts on my phone.
One from Audrey, "Where are you?"
One from Dad, "I have a surprise for you.
Get your skinny butt home."

I go.
Slow steps.
Trees sway,
Waving goodbye
For now.
My oak.
I pause,
Lean in, and
Place my body,
My face,
Against its bark
And breathe in.

Wood,
Earth,
Something real.
That's all I want,
Something real.
I have
Someone real
In Audrey.

A car sits in my driveway, and
I struggle to recognize it.
As I head up the walkway
Towards the front door,
I hear Peter talking to someone,
A woman's voice that I recognize.
It sounds weaker than I remember
From a few months ago after
Mom died,
And I pause before entering
The house,
Hearing Peter say,
"Mom says hello."
"Oh, really." Grandma's voice.
I gather Peter is telling Grandma that he
Talks to Mom and gets to visit her often.
Mom must spend all of her time with Peter
Because I haven't seen her or heard from her.

I walk in,
Grandma on the couch,

Peter next to her,
Dad in his recliner,
And then he appears
From the kitchen,
A glass of water in hand.
My heart races,
Skin flushed.
Weakened by emotion,
I almost fall.
I feel a deep filth in my
Bones.
The cleansing from the creek has come
Undone,
And I suddenly
Regret my
Nakedness
With him so near,
In the same state.
Uncle Kipp,
Standing in my house.
I want to scream,
And I am, but it's all in
My head.
I want to run into the kitchen,
Grab a knife,
And introduce it to his belly.
My nemesis,
My rapist,
Who stole my innocence,
My thoughts.

Who stole everything
Pure,
My confidence.
Who stole my life,
My breath.

Grandma reaches for my hand,
Startles my thoughts,
And I pull away.
Dad looks at me, curious
As to my reaction.
I try to hide my
Fear,
Frustration,
With Kipp so near.
I turn and hug Grandma.
"You've grown," she says,
Looking up,
"Hasn't he, Kipp?"
Uncle Kipp looks me up and down,
Sizing me up.
His eyes looking at me
Makes me want to
Vomit all over the floor.
"You need to eat more," says Grandma.
"Nothing but skin and bones."
I feel his stare deep in
My bones,
And as for my skin,
I want to peel it off,

Which I'm surprised hasn't happened
By now
With how hard and often
I scrub my body,
Trying to wash away
The feeling of his
Body.
"Yeah." Kipp nods.
"You could use a few pounds."

"So, what are you doing here?"
I try not to sound mean for
Grandma's sake,
But my tone is direct and
My voice is somewhat shaky.
Dad speaks up, not sure if he's
Catching on to my uncomfortableness.
"They are here for your graduation."
Dad looks over at Grandma.
"That's a long drive just for that," I say.
"I offered to fly your grandma, but
Kipp said he would drive her," Dad responds.
Uncle Kipp smiles at me.
I can't see his smile directly, but
I can see It from the
Corner of my eye,
Feel It in my soul.
Kipp is just an "It" to me.
The disgust he brings me is
Making my skin

Tingle,
My vision
Blur,
My breathing
Increase.
Palms sweating,
Panic attack
On its way.
Fuck!
"I'll be right back."
I go toward my room.
"Don't be long," says Kipp.
His words are like
Hot liquid in my ears.
I want to kill him,
Avenge my twelve-year-old self.
I can't.
I find myself in my room,
Trying to breathe like
Mom and Prudence taught me.
I'm suffocating in fear
And humiliation,
Holding my knees
Against my chest.
Hugging my fear,
My loss.
Which is me.
Lost.

FORTY-FIVE

I am forced to reconcile
With my younger self
As the man who stole him
Sits before me,
Eating a chicken dinner.
Licking the grease
From his dirty fingers.
The same fingers
That once fondled me,
Held me,
Restrained me,
Raped me.

Audrey has called twice, and
I finally text her.
"I'll call later. Sorry!
There's a story. Love you!"
"K," she replies.
I couldn't bear having
Her meet him,
Uncle Kipp,
The man who
Raped me.
If she heard
His name,
Saw his face,
It would either

Trigger
Her own emotions
About her
Rape,
Or she might actually try
To rip his eyes from his skull,
Like she said she would
If she ever met him.

Night lingers on,
Kipp taking smoke breaks,
Grandma taking wine breaks,
Dad trying his best to be
A good son-in-law,
Though Mom never really
Liked her mother.
Mom used to say, "She's controlling."
Peter is watching *Star Trek*,
Having a marathon.
School's out.
I suddenly fear for him,
Wondering if Kipp
Ever raped him too.
Not knowing if Peter would
Understand.
My rage is growing
For a man who will
Sleep under the
Same roof as me,
Something that hasn't happened

In almost six years
Because we stopped visiting
After Mom and Grandma had a
Falling out.
Now they are here,
And I need to escape.

"I'm going to stay at TJ's tonight," I say.
"Tomorrow is graduation," says Dad.
"Yeah, we won't be up late.
We had it planned for a while."
"You need to get your rest," says Grandma.
"I'm just walking on a stage and
Grabbing a piece of paper."
Grandma looks at me with a frown.
"You need to take this seriously.
You only graduate once.
In fact, you should go to bed soon."
Dad looks at me, almost
Pleading with his eyes, but I
Plead back with mine.
"Okay, tell TJ to get you home
In time to get ready." Dad smiles.
Kipp comes in from his smoke break.
"Where you off to?"
I struggle to
Comprehend the words
That come from his
Filthy mouth.
Fear will do that.

Anxiety will seize your brain of
All thought.
Trauma will send your head
Spinning and weigh down your shoulders
And crush your chest.
Grandma says, "You should answer him."
Then she looks at my dad. "He's changed."
Staring up at me, she finishes,
"You are quite disrespectful not answering your elders."
I keep it simple. "A friend."
I see why Mom decided to stay away.
"Go ahead, son," says Dad,
"Have fun with TJ, and we will see you tomorrow."
I can tell Dad is growing irritated with his visitors.

I leave the house,
A sleeping bag
Under my arm.
Not heading to TJ's,
Going to see Audrey
To get lost
In her eyes.
Salvation.

FORTY-SIX

We meet at the path.
I didn't realize I'd be back here
So quickly,
But being under the trees
Next to the creek
With someone I love
And trust
Is what I need.

I wait until we're seated
Next to the water
To tell her what is going on.
To tell her that I faced my rapist
And swallowed my words,
Choking on them
From fear.
Am I a coward?

"That motherfucker is here?" Audrey becomes irate.
I nod, pulling my knees closer to my chest.
"They arrived today for graduation,"
I say as my breathing increases.
"I haven't seen or heard from my grandma since
Mom's funeral. It's strange why they are here now."
Audrey moves closer,
Her warmth against me
As she sees me white-knuckle my knees.

"Are you okay?" she asks.
"I was worried about telling you," I say,
"I didn't want it to upset you."
"It does upset me. It should upset me."
She's right.
Facing a pedophile,
A rapist,
Should be upsetting.

We lie back,
Letting the wind brush over
Our faces
And hearts
And capture our minds.
I want the wind to take
My thoughts and let them
Drift
To a different place,
One that is far away.
However, with my thoughts
Spinning,
It would turn into a tornado
Wiping out a village.
I am cursed by memory.

"How long are they here?" asks Audrey.
"Three days," I say.
Audrey shakes her head and sighs.
"That fucker has nerve,
Coming here, showing his rapist face."

I sit up, throwing stones into the creek,
And as I look down,
It seems the stones are vanishing.
Only the dirt floor of the woods remains.
For years, the creek has received the rocks
I've thrown,
And for some reason,
This saddens me,
Like something is coming to an end.
Maybe my time for letting go is here,
Next to the creek,
My sanctuary.
My need to let go of my trauma
Before it ruins me completely.
At least accept it.
Trauma like ours is permanent.
It's how we live and cope with it
That truly matters.
Acceptance
Of what happened
Is key
For understanding.
Acceptance
Is key,
Knowing that I was
Once happy,
And with Audrey,
I am once again
Happy.
Acceptance.

As the evening becomes cooler,
I spread out my sleeping bag
And build a small fire in
The same stone ring that
Our dads had built for prom,
The ash still there from burnt wood,
A memory.
All ash is a memory that is either
Happy or tragic.
My mind is
Burnt in memory.

"Will your parents be worried about you?" I ask.
"No, they think I'm at a friend named Amber's house."
"You don't have a friend named Amber," I say,
"In fact, you don't have any girlfriends."
I smile.
"Asshole." She nudges me.
"Maybe that will change
In New York, after I get away from this town."
I nod, still not accepting that I'm going too.
It seems unreal, maybe too big,
Too much, too soon,
And too overwhelming.
"I can't wait to get out of here," she says, facing the creek.
"I'm happy that you're finding
A new place, a new start."
"Oh, it's a new start, but
I'll still carry all the shit I deal with now
Even though I'll be a thousand miles away.

I'm not naive that it'll just go away.
Memories are stuck
Like honey to arm hair."
"That's kinda gross," I say.
"Well, my memories are gross."
"Yeah, you're right. Stupid thing to say."
Audrey continues, "Your memories are too."
I agree with a nod.
"For both of us to have so much taken from us,
To feel that kind of pain and for the people that caused
It to just be walking around free, probably still doing it.
Who knows how many girls that fucker has raped at
        parties."
Audrey pauses, and a single tear falls.
Silence,
Because sometimes tears deserve quiet.
"Like your rapist. He's in your house right now.
Eating your fucking food, sleeping under your fucking
        roof.
He's free. How many little boys has he raped?"
My breath leaves me suddenly when she says that.
Audrey feels it.
Sees it.
And then holds me tight.
Not letting go, knowing I'm so close to tears,
Panic,
And the thought of Kipp raping other little boys.
I want him dead.
I want every part of him dead.
So he can't ever harm anyone again.

So he can't take another boy's innocence.
So he can't ruin another boy's memories.
So he can't steal another boy's soul
And provide him with secrets
That he has to carry around
Like a thousand-pound pack
On his shoulders,
Never getting rid of it,
Just walking through life
Weighted down
Daily.

We lie there next to the fire,
The night fading.
More light this time of year
As the sun is
Still hanging on,
Trickling through the trees.
The water running next to us,
Holding all my stones,
My stories,
Suffering with me.
Audrey leans in.
We hold each other.
We hold each other's memories.
We hold each other's fears.
And we hold each other together
Because together we are strong.
We are whole.

We don't make love
As we have come to do
In our sanctuary.
Love cannot be made
When so much talk of assault
Has been lingering in the air,
Sorrow taking our spirit
But not our hearts
As they beat next to each other.
Love has found us.
New memories are being made.
New stones will be found
And tossed.

FORTY-SEVEN

I find myself in a red gown,
Standing in line
Surrounded by strangers,
Students I walked the halls with
But never knew.
All of us
Will become memories
Or faces on social media.
We wait to enter the fieldhouse and
Walk in single file
To our assigned seats
Like we rehearsed.
We had practiced the
Pre-ceremonial march,
A march to freedom,
For what seemed like fifty times.
The principal, in his three-piece,
Preaching from the podium,
Fake words, as if he knows us.
It's his day to shine, and he didn't want us
Screwing up in front of
His audience.

After we sit in our metal chairs,
I find TJ
Staring blankly three rows up.
And Audrey,

Behind me to my left,
Her hair hanging perfectly
Around her shoulders.
I can still
Feel her softness
On my hands from
Last night, simply holding
Her tight.
Dad in the bleachers,
Peter by his side,
And Grandma,
And Kipp.
My chest starts to ache
And feels heavy,
Like an elephant is sitting
On it, trying to crush me.
Just the sight of Kipp seems
To paralyze me.

Speeches about our future.
Speeches about life.
Speeches about never giving up.
There must be a book
"How to write a graduation speech."
They are all the same,
Trying to inspire,
But only leaving me
Feeling more
Alone.
We walk like cattle

To gather
Pieces of paper
From men I hardly know.
The crowd erupting for their
Students.
The students erupting for the
Popular kids,
Especially the one who threw
The secret grad party.
My grad party was with Audrey
Next to a creek,
Under the stars.

We are all seated.
Uneventful.
It's over,
And now home
For catered food
And catered
Conversation,
Faking it.
All I can think about
Is Mom
And Kipp,
And I hate myself
For including both
Of them in the same
Thought.
I wish I could crush
My brain.

FORTY-EIGHT

TJ drives me home.
"I'll be back at eight
After my dinner!" he screams
Over the music coming
From his car.
I give a nod to tell
Him I acknowledge what
He said.
Sometimes it seems like
A nod is my greatest form
Of communication.

I hear laughter in my house,
And I suddenly regret entering
Through the front doors
Where I will have to act like
I'm happy.
Then, I hear a familiar voice,
Not one, but two voices
That calm my nerves enough
To walk inside and face Kipp,
Be in the same room as Kipp.
It's two voices that
Have entered my headspace before
And bring with it a sense of
Self-worth,

Self-efficacy,
And safety.

I try to enter silently
Without being noticed,
Like I do everywhere I go,
But a small room with a
Creaky door does not allow
For stealthy moves.
A room of people,
Clapping.
"There's the graduate," says Dad.
He comes to me and hugs me.
I almost lose it right then and there
Because behind him,
Looking at me, is Kipp,
And he winks as
I hug my dad.
He fucking winks at me.
Peter lifts me from the floor.
"My brother is smart," he says
As he holds my diploma.
I gave it to him right after graduation,
And Peter held it tight,
And now he hands it to me.
"To my brother, Dylan, for being
Smart."
That means more than Principal
What's-His-Name giving it to me.
Next is Grandma. "Well, I think

Your mom would be proud." And then
A slight kiss on the cheek.
Prudence is in front of me after Grandma.
It's like being on a
Merry-go-round,
Spinning with kisses and hugs
And voices.
"Dylan, I am so proud of you," says Prudence.
"You have come so far. I'm simply...impressed."
Then Kipp, coming toward me,
Right hand out
To shake mine.
Everything within me is holding back,
My head screaming, "Fuck no! Don't do it!"
Kipp stands there, looking me in the eye,
Except this time we are level
Instead of when I was a twelve-year-old boy,
Having to look up at him,
Or when he raped me and I had to look
Facedown at the ground.
I am stuck,
Frozen,
So he reaches for
My hand and takes
It in his,
Forcing the action.
I can't think, and for a moment I feel
Like I might pass out.
Dizzy.
Breathing.

Paralyzed.

Dying inside.

"I'm proud of you" is what

I think Kipp says.

He backs away and then

Mr. Johnson hugs me.

He holds me tight for a moment

And then eases back.

"You okay?"

I'm screaming in my head,

"Fuck no! I am not okay!

Save me!

Kill me!

Kill him!"

I think for a split second that

All of those words had come out of me, but

The room is normal,

Everyone talking, getting ready to eat.

"Hey, do you need to talk?" asks Mr. Johnson.

I want to tell him.

If anyone, I want him to know

That this man,

Standing in my living room,

Eating my food,

Touching my hand,

Raped me.

I just shake my head,

Which seems heavy

And my neck tight when

I move it to say, "No."

Mr. Johnson lets me go,
But stays near
As we eat pulled pork sandwiches
And coleslaw
With corn on the cob,
My favorite.
Dad ordered it special
For me, but I can
Barely stomach
A bite and really want to
Vomit all over.

My height has changed,
So has my voice,
But not my eyes.
They see truth
And create memory,
Leaving me wanting to
Tear them out
One by one.
To be blind from pain,
Though lack of sight
Would not end the suffering,
But an absence of heart would.
Having no memory might help,
But instead, my memory is a sharp
Ice pick lodged in my brain.

And then my heart,
My reason,

Walks through the front door,
The evening sun
Bringing out her auburn hair
As if it's on fire.
Our eyes meet,
The green eyes
That I have swum in
A thousand times,
Calming me,
Getting lost
Within.
And she comes to me
As if floating,
Flying even,
And my face must say,
"Take me away,"
Because she does,
As her hand takes mine,
The same hand that Kipp held,
And now it feels clean again,
Pure,
All from her touch.
She guides me
To my room
And closes the door.
It seems like maybe
We are invisible,
Like Audrey has a magic shield
Around us,
Because no one notices.

"Are you okay?" asks Audrey.

"I'm trying to be," I say.

"You know..." Audrey steps over

To my window, arms folded.

Her jean shorts curve with her figure,

And the dark-blue t-shirt

Fits against her lean back,

And I suddenly have the urge to

Kiss her, take her to the creek,

And make love.

Instead, I wait and listen.

"Maybe we shouldn't have to try.

Maybe it's okay our minds are a mess.

After all, look at what we've been through.

The ones that did this to us...

They shouldn't be okay."

I sit on my bed. "Yeah, you're right."

I lie back on my pillow and

Stare at the ceiling where I have a poster

Of The Smiths that has been there since I was thirteen.

"Prudence once talked about karma, you know,

What goes around comes around.

Maybe something is coming their way."

I look over at her, still staring

Out the window,

And add, "I know Kipp has been busted for three OWIs,

And lost his job."

Audrey turns. "You really think that's karma for a fucking

Low-life rapist?"

And she's right.
It isn't.

She finds her way next to my pillow
And looks up. "Good band," she says.
"I suppose we should go back to your party."
Audrey reaches for my hand and
Gently places hers on top.
"I guess I'll have to try to not rip your uncle's face off."
We both chuckle, and I turn my head to the right
To find her eyes a few inches from mine.
We pause, no words,
Only shallow breathing,
And I move toward her and
Close the slight gap
And wait until she comes the rest of the way.
We softly kiss.
Then she looks back at my ceiling, and to the
Window and door.
"What are you doing?" I ask.
"You know, this will be about as big as our
Entire apartment
In New York,
Except a bathroom and small kitchen will
Fit into the same space."
We laugh
And I roll my body into hers.
"We don't need anything else."

We walk slowly back to the living room,
Into the kitchen,
And then outside to where
Peter is telling Mr. Johnson about
The last episode of *Star Trek*.
Prudence is talking with Dad.
Grandma is napping in her chair.
Kipp is gone.
I don't want to ask.
I don't want to because then
I'll have to say his name, and even the thought
Of those words coming from my mouth,
As if I cared about where he is,
Makes me nauseous.

Dad sees me scanning the yard.
"Your uncle went to get more beer," he says,
"Apparently a six-pack wasn't enough."
Then, all at once, it seems everyone looks up.
"Audrey!"
She smiles and blushes as her name comes from so many,
And it startles Grandma awake for a moment.
"Hey, let's open gifts," says Dad.
Grandma must have just been resting her eyes
Because she heard everything and promptly says,
"Not without Kipp."
"Oh, we can show him later," Dad says as he gets
A dirty look from Grandma.
Dad adds, "Maybe by then he'll sober up."
Grandma leans forward, about to say something,

And then Peter chimes in,
A square box with *Star Trek* wrapping paper,
"Here's your gift, Dylan."
"Is this from you?" I ask.
"Yep, it's a Captain..."
Peter stops himself from telling me.
I tear open the paper like I'm more excited
Than anything to see what's in it. Peter smiles
With pride as he watches. It's a t-shirt with
Captain Kirk on it, and it reads "Beam Me Up, Scotty."
Prudence is next to hand me a gift.
I unwrap it slowly and say,
"You really shouldn't
Have gotten me anything.
Yoga is enough."
It's a bracelet that reads "Namaste" on top
And "Make your own way" on the bottom.
I put it on immediately, securing it to my wrist.
"Thank you!"
Mr. Johnson is next and hands me an item
That's clearly a book wrapped in all-blue paper.
I have never had a teacher give me a present or
Come over to my house. I have never had a teacher
Who I connected with, and I'm almost hesitant
To open his gift, not wanting to rush the moment.
It's actually two books,
Twenty Love Poems and
A Song of Despair by Pablo Neruda,
The Alchemist by Paulo Coelho.
"Thanks so much." I give Mr. Johnson a fist bump,

Probably one of my last, and say,
"I'm sure they will be great."
"Keep them handy and read them slow," he says.
Dad steps over and hands me a gift bag with
An envelope, and then he leans in.
"I love you!"
Is all he says.
The envelope has a message,
A letter,
Handwritten
From Mom.

Holding her words,
Touching a piece of paper
That she held in her
Dying hands,
Makes me feel
Connected to her.
I place the paper
Against my chest,
Not able to look
At the words yet.
And as tears start,
I put the note in
My pocket,
Not wanting the
Water from my eyes
To fall and smudge
The ink
That holds Mom's

Message to me.
For now,
I will save it
For the creek.

No one says anything.
They don't demand I read it,
Even Grandma,
Knowing that what a dying mother
Says to her grieving son
Is personal,
And then Dad hands me a gift.
I open it slowly, still fighting
Full-blown crying and not
Wanting to break down,
Wondering what Mom said to me,
And then I look at the picture
Before me
In a frame
That says,
Take The Road Less Traveled.
In the purple frame
Is a picture of Mom holding me
As a baby.
One I haven't seen before.
She's so young
And beautiful,
Strong!
There is no cancer,
Nothing stopping her,

With a life ahead of her
And a son that she would mentor,
And another that she would celebrate
His abilities and not his disabilities,
And a husband who she would hold
Together, and ground, and love
Without judgment.
And suddenly Dad is holding me,
Peter is holding us,
And as Dad and I cry, looking at
The woman who was our rock,
Peter says, "Mom says congratulations."
Dad and I smile as Peter is smashing us
Together, our faces inches apart.
His strength never ceases to amaze me.

I pass around the picture,
And everyone is gentle
When they hold it
As if it's the most fragile item
On Earth.
But they are smiling,
Pleasant.
Prudence puts her hands together
And says, "Namaste," as she looks down
At Mom in her lap.
Mr. Johnson simply says,
"True beauty, both of you."
Audrey whispers, "I wish I could have met you."
And Grandma shakes her head and is quiet,

But her eyes flood as she excuses herself
And walks into the house.

Mom has always had an impact
In life and in death,
In person and in a picture frame,
Because people that are real,
True to themselves
And true to others,
Will always have an impact.

Prudence and Mr. Johnson say goodbye.
I will see Prudence again in a class
For certain,
But as I hug Mr. Johnson,
I'm not sure if I will ever be in his
Presence in this lifetime.
It's one thing that I find sad about life,
That people come into our little worlds,
Stay for a while, and then leave.
It's just part of our journey,
And only a few stay for the duration.
As I hug him goodbye,
He says, "Remember, those that
Wander
Are not lost."
And I suddenly realize that the entire time
That Mr. Johnson was teaching us,
Sharing poems and books and quotes
And stories and his own experiences,

He was actually talking to
Himself,
About
Himself,
Encouraging us through
Himself,
Always giving us a piece of
Himself
To take with us and ponder,
And for those lessons
I will be eternally grateful.
And then he is gone.

Life is about loss,
Losing those that pass by
One way or another,
Drifting in and out of our world
To hold a place in our memory,
Whether alive or dead.
They are there,
A thought away,
And we can reach them
Anytime we want,
If only for a moment,
To smile upon their faces
And be next to them again.
A memory can haunt us,
But a memory can free us
From sorrow
If we allow it to.

FORTY-NINE

TJ picks us up and
We all go to Bridges.
It might sound lame to
Spend your graduation
Night at a coffee shop, but
None of us party.
Bridges has a special
Night for graduates,
Staying open until midnight,
Live folk music on their tiny stage,
Acoustic guitars covering
Bob Dylan
And a few originals.
It's a night for us,
Three friends celebrating
With our lives in front of us,
A milestone reached,
Grasped, and then let go,
On our way to whatever is next.

TJ takes the stage.
A young woman
In her early twenties
Comes and stands by him,
Guitar in hand,
Strap around her neck.
TJ leans into the mic.

I look at Audrey,
Not knowing what he's doing
Or about to say.
With TJ, you just don't know.
"This is for my best friend,
Dylan.
He's been my brother
Since we were eight,
And I love him for it."

I'm taken aback.
Audrey holds my hand.
TJ sings all the time
In his car, or at his house,
Or when we chill,
And it's usually something
Mellow,
But I have never seen him
Sing on a stage
With an audience.
And with his humor,
Dry and bold,
I'm actually a little
Scared what words may
Come from his mouth
About me,
His "brother."
I agree,
We are brothers.

The woman starts a chord.
TJ begins singing my favorite
Song,
"Bob Dylan's Dream,"
And as he sings out
The lyrics,
The verse,
"How many a year has passed and gone
Many a gamble has been lost and won
And many a road taken by many a first friend
And each one I've never seen again."
I realize TJ is
Saying goodbye
In his own way,
And when a tear falls gently
From my eye to my cheek,
I leave it there
Because some tears aren't meant
To be dried and taken away.
I have a friend on stage
Singing to me,
A new love sitting against me,
And I realize,
Even with all the suffering,
That I am lucky,
Fortunate,
To have a life where people
Are genuine
And care.

TJ finishes.
The patrons
Clap.
He bows
And then leans
Into the mic.
The crowd hushes.
"My friend, Dylan,
His mom named
Him after the man who
Wrote and sang that song,
Bob Dylan."
TJ takes a step back.
He seems like he needs
A moment
To clear his throat,
Compose himself.
"His mom,
The greatest of moms,
Passed away
Several months ago,
And I hope she heard this tonight."

I hug TJ,
Our moment,
As Audrey sits back
Smiling upon our friendship.
Two awkward kids,
Emerging men
That know each other's

Secrets,
Dreams,
And then TJ says,
"Okay, I'm going home.
You guys good?"
Audrey and I laugh
Because that's TJ,
Random as hell,
And I love him for it.

We walk tonight,
The warmth of June air
On our faces.
Nights like these,
Where the stars fill the sky
And the moon seems closer,
The air heavy,
And Audrey does what I love most.
She hangs on to the inside of
My elbow as we walk.
Nights like these
Need to be savored.

"The creek?" she suggests.
I simply nod and
Steer us in
That direction.
As we walk, a few cars pass,
Honk, and graduates yell
From their windows,

Mostly just cheers,
And we wave back.
Then, Aaron drives by,
Close to the sidewalk,
And slows.
He's alone,
So I don't worry
Too much.
Bullies,
Cowards,
Do not do much alone.
Nevertheless, I
Block his view of Audrey
With my body,
Trying to look as broad
And as big as I can.

His car stops completely.
Audrey pulls me to walk.
"Let's just keep going," she says.
"Hold on. Let's see what he wants," I reply.
I take a step forward, wanting him to know
I'm not afraid.
I am tired of being afraid.
Aaron sits looking at me
For just a moment, but it feels
Like several minutes,
An uncomfortable stare.
I'm now ready to go because it
Seems like he's plotting,

And then he gets out.
I am ready
To fight
And calmly tell Audrey,
"Get ready to run."
She says, "Fuck that.
I'm going to
Rip his throat out."
Oddly, my confidence grows knowing
That the two of us could take him easily.
Standing by the front of his car,
Aaron speaks.
"Hey, ummm...I just wanted to apologize...I..."
Audrey and I look at each other
As if checking to see if what's happening
Is real or not, and then
I look back at Aaron,
A boy who seems to be
Struggling with words.
He continues, "What I did was pretty messed up."
He is looking at Audrey.
"I should have never grabbed you."
Audrey doesn't respond.
I'm skeptical if this is real, true,
Waiting
For him to pounce.
"I mean, fuck, after I grabbed you, and
After our fight,
I thought,
I'm becoming my dad.

That fucking prick."
I can tell, right now, that this boy,
Athletic, popular, handsome kid,
Is suffering too.
Maybe not like us,
But suffering with his own
Darkness.
"Anyhow, I don't want to be like that anymore.
I'm getting the hell out of here,
Going to Nebraska to play football for four years.
I guess it's a way to pay for school."
I smile at him and say,
"Good luck, Aaron."
He steps closer,
Reaches his hand out.
I take it,
A truce.
"Take care of yourselves,"
Aaron says to both of us,
And then he leaves,
Driving slowly down the road.
Audrey and I watch until he turns
And his taillights are out of view.

We continue to walk to the path,
Her hand back around my elbow,
Quietly processing what just occurred,
And then Audrey breaks the silence.
"Well, that was unexpected," she says.
"I guess people can change

If they want to," I reply.
"Yeah, like he said, he didn't want to
Be like his dad. Maybe that is
Motivation enough."

We walk toward the full moon
That I think we could reach
If we walked another mile.
It lights the path
And the field as we stroll,
Stopping at our oak tree
To perform our ritual
Hug.
Audrey holds it
Just a few more moments,
Her face against the bark,
And I come around and kiss
Her cheek, making her smile.
She turns,
Taking me into her arms,
Holding me tight,
Tighter than the tree.
I never want to let her go,
Or for her to let me go.
I have come to find comfort in her touch
And home in her arms.
It makes me feel
Safe,
Wanted,
Loved.

We make our way to the creek
And lie down on an area
That seems to remember our bodies.
We don't say a word
As I guide my hands over her
And she does the same.
I have the contours of her body memorized,
The places she likes to be touched.
I have learned the way she likes to be kissed,
Slow, with meaning,
And our bodies move in harmony.
The light that trickles
Through the trees
Glows
On her skin.
I kiss every part of her,
Taking in
All of her,
And then we quietly
Fall asleep as I hold her,
My love, in my arms,
Her head upon my chest,
Gentle water flowing.

FIFTY

I walk Audrey home
The next morning.
We agree to sleep
And then see each other later
To start planning New York,
Our future,
Whatever that means.
The thought that we will be together
Is the only reassurance
I need.
As she leaves,
She turns and
Looks at me
Like she knows something
I don't
And says,
"Stay gold, Ponyboy."

I walk the familiar sidewalks
That have felt my feet since I was a kid,
Realizing that in just a couple of months,
I will no longer walk them.
I will no longer be coming home
From my creek, my path.
Instead, I will have to find a new path.

I enter my house.
Quiet.
Silence.
Walk into the kitchen
To the smell of coffee
And toast,
Uncle Kipp at the table
Just staring at the black liquid,
Obviously hungover.
My chest becomes immediately
Tight,
Hurting,
Heavy.
After being with
Audrey last night,
I had somehow
Forgotten,
Or maybe
Hoped,
That he and
Grandma would be
Gone.
Audrey has always helped me
Forget my pain,
But here he is,
My rapist,
Sitting at my table,
And I again am frozen.
Fear!
Rage!

"Hey, Dylan," he says.
I become nauseous as my name
Vomits from his mouth.
It almost seems like a
Dirty word,
Filthy.
I look around and
Out the window
For the others.
"They went to breakfast,
And then to see your
Mom's grave.
Your dad left a note."
I want to run from the house
And back to Audrey or to
Mom's grave.
It's what the therapist called
My "flight" response.
I want to go, but then
I feel anger,
Rage.
Fist clenched,
Neck tight,
And then
Fury.
I jump on top of Kipp,
Punching his face
As hard as I can,
Getting my blows in,
Stunning him.

But Kipp is strong,
He is trained,
And he took me down.

I find myself below him,
My stomach to the floor,
His body heavy on me,
Grossly familiar.
I'm screaming in my head,
"*Not again!*"
I struggle to fight him,
But the more I move my thin arms,
The tighter his grip becomes
And the heavier he feels,
His breath warm on the side of my face
And the smell of stale beer
Seeping from his breath.
"You little fucker." He pushes his
Mouth to my right ear.
"What the hell do you think you're doing?"
I can hardly get enough air in my lungs to yell,
And all I can get out is
"You fucking rapist!"
"You still blame me for something so
Long ago?
You wanted it as
Much as I did."
Kipp starts to kiss my face and neck, and I
Try to kick him off, but can't.
If I could get free, I would

Grab a knife and put
It through his belly.
But he is heavy, and
I'm getting tired
From his strength holding me and
My adrenaline leaving me.
Exhausted.
Giving up.
Fear.
Panic!
For a single moment,
The thought enters my head
That I can't handle this again.
Not at my age,
Almost a man,
Fully grown
And not able to defend myself.
I know I will kill myself
Afterward.
Giving up,
Voice gone,
Kipp starts to place his hands
All over me,
And then Audrey comes
Rolling into
My head,
My vision.
Mom is there too,
And Prudence,
TJ,

Mr. Johnson,
Peter,
Dad.
And even though I still
Can't
Break free,
I raise my head and chest
High enough
That a noise leaves me like I
Never thought I was capable of,
And I scream,
"No! Fuck no!
HELP ME!
ANYONE!
PLEASE!"
I plead.
And then, as I know she is
Listening,
Like Peter always says,
I scream one more time,
"MOM!"

My energy has completely left me now.
Kipp becomes heavier,
But then noise explodes
All around me.
Kipp is lifted off his feet,
Into the air,
Thrown against the table.
I am dazed,

Blurred,
Like I'm waking up
From a dream.
"Peter," I gasp.
Peter stands over me.
Strong.
"Stay away from my brother!" he yells.
And as Kipp moves toward Peter,
I see Dad enter the kitchen
And grab Kipp,
Throwing him against the wall.
He takes Kipp's throat and
Squeezes the breath from him.
"I'll fucking kill you if you touch
My kids."
Kipp's strength is
No match for Dad.
He can't even move and
Stops trying.

Grandma looks down at me
Lying on the kitchen floor,
Belt undone.
I always wear a belt
Tight.
It's for security,
But anything can be
Undone.
Grandma gasps.
"What are you doing, Dylan?"

And then to my dad,
"Get your hands off of him."
I am silent,
Stunned.
Dad slowly lets Kipp go
From the choke hold.
Kipp, trying to take
Deep breaths.
His breath,
Disgusting
Over my neck,
Brings back my
Twelve-year-old
Self
With his breath
All over my
Body.
Grandma reaches for Kipp.
"Get your things," she says.
Kipp leaves the kitchen.
Dad looks at Grandma.
"You've got to be kidding me.
He's not going anywhere until the
Police talk to him."
"He's family," says Grandma.
"Well, our definition of 'family' is
Different." Dad comes to lift me to
My feet.
Peter stands close
And hugs me

Tight.
"He just needs help," says Grandma.
"He has a problem."

Grandma condoning
Kipp's "problem,"
Making excuses
For his "problem."
She knows
About Kipp's "problem"?
My life has been
Ruined
Because of this "problem,"
And then words come from my mouth,
Out from my thoughts.
"Fuck his problem."
I have never sworn at my grandma,
Or any adult.
Mom wouldn't have liked that,
But Kipp's "problem" stole my
Soul,
So this one time,
I think Mom would approve.

Dad pulls me close
As if to say,
"*Let me handle this.*"
Kipp is in the car
Honking the horn.
Grandma walks briskly

To the vehicle,
Faster than I've ever seen
Her move.
"I want to kill him," I say to no one.
I hear the car back out and then drive away.
Another rapist getting away
And it being condoned
Because he has a "problem,"
As Grandma stated.

Fuck his problem.
His problem caused
My darkness,
My pain.
Stole my childhood,
My teenage years,
My life.
Swirled my
Childhood around,
Making me want
To produce my own death
Multiple times,
Year after year.
So his problem
Can go to hell.

Peter comes to Dad and me,
Pulls us in tight,
Strong.
His arms squeeze us

And then he says loudly,
"The Avengers took care of him."
Dad and I laugh as Peter
Smothers us in a hug
That brings us face-to-face,
And Dad says, "Which Avengers are we?"
Peter pulls back, flexes his arms and shoulders.
"I'm Hulk, Dad is Thor, and Dylan is Captain
America."
We laugh.
I step closer to Peter,
Looking down at my big brother,
My avenger,
And say, "Buddy, you are my hero."

Peter goes to watch *Star Trek*.
I know he'll be busy with
Kirk and Spock
For hours.
I sit across from Dad at the
Kitchen table, and
I confess everything.
Confess?
What a word,
Usually spoken by the guilty
And by victims.
"I was just a boy," I start.
Dad's eyes become darker
As the conversation continues,
But he needs to hear this.

He needs to feel the
Weight
That his son has been
Carrying
With him for years.
"He forced me down,
Took everything from me on
That mountain.
Everything!"
I hold my head for a moment
But I do not cry.
I'm not sure
I have tears left in me.
I have drained them all
From years of shedding them,
Or maybe I refuse to cry
Because I realize
it gives Kipp power
Over me,
And I want
Control
Back in my life,
To start living.
The load I carry is no less,
Just moving forward.
Resilience!

Dad's tears are plenty.
He has questions and needs answers.
"Did your mom know?"

I shake my head and reply,
"It would have killed her,
Or she would have killed him."
We smirk at that.
"Why didn't you tell me?"
I think for a moment,
And the question almost seems
Like it places blame on me,
Because that's what
"Why" questions do.
I know.
I have asked them for five years,
And "why" questions
Tear your guts out.
So do "what-ifs."
"I couldn't." I clear my throat.
"I wish you would have," says Dad.
"You would have killed him," I say,
Then continue, "And then I'd be without
A mom or a dad."
He nods in agreement and says,
"Dylan, I'm doing everything I can right now
Not to chase down his car and
Kill him on the highway."
"I know," I say,
"I have thought about killing him myself.
TJ wanted to do it too."
Dad looks at me blankly.
"I wouldn't have expected that."
I'm not sure if he means me or TJ

That he wouldn't have expected that from.
"Dad, I was just too embarrassed.
It was as if he took away
My boyhood,
My youth,
Becoming
A man,
Being a man.
My strength.
Everything.
I just locked it up
And placed it in a vault."
Survival.
He acknowledges how I felt.
"Does anyone besides TJ know?"
"Audrey," I say,
"She wanted to kill him too." I chuckle.
"Now that doesn't surprise me," says Dad,
"You hang on to her."
I sit back, staring out the kitchen window.
The humidity is thick, the air still, and
The trees green.
"I love her," I tell him,
"I love her so much it scares me."
"Have you told her?" Dad asks.
"A thousand times.
We don't hide anything from each other.
We share our dreams, our fears."
Dad looks down at the table as if he's
Studying it.

"I miss that," he says.
He doesn't need to say anything else.
In our silence,
I think for a moment
How strange this
Life is.
Our conversation has gone from
Murdering a rapist to
The loves of our lives.

"Dad." I break the silence.
"Yeah." He looks up, waiting.
"I don't want you to feel guilty."
"That's incredibly hard.
A father
Is here
To protect
His son."
"I know, but by loving me,
You, Mom, and Peter..." I pause.
"By loving me unconditionally,
Always being there,
Being my father,
It's saved me.
You are..." I stop to gather my breath.
"You are what a man should be."
And then he grabs me,
Pulling me into his muscled chest,
Holding me. "I love you so much,"
He says softly. "You are my life."

We hear "Beam me up, Scotty"
In the background
And break into laughter.
Our Hulk,
Our savior,
In his room,
Full of strength.
Literally.
"I think we should press charges," says Dad.
His tone turns serious.
He looks directly at me.
"He needs to pay,
If not by my hand, then by the law."
I think for a moment how long I have wanted
Revenge,
How much I have wanted
Justice,
And then simply say, "No."
Dad is taken aback.
"Dylan, that son of a bitch is a
Rapist.
You heard your grandma. 'His problem.'
He's a pedophile
And needs to be stopped."
I fold my arms against my body,
My fear and anxiety building,
Moving from tingling in my feet
To my hands,
Chest,
And into my face.

Kipp has already
Taken so much from me.
If I turn him in,
Tell my story,
What else
Will be taken?
"I'm just...too embarrassed.
I don't want the world
Knowing what happened.
I already feel like a freak."
Dad moves closer. He takes my hands.
I look at our hands grasped together.
Mine are his.
I have my father's hands,
My mother's eyes.
"Dylan." Dad leans in further.
"My son, you are my blood, and
When you hurt,
I hurt.
Our pain is the same.
I cannot take it away from you,
But I can help you carry it,
Experience it."
Dad is now crying as he hugs me.
"You were right not to tell your mother.
This would have crushed her.
She never liked Kipp and always said
Something was wrong with him."
Then he rises up, wipes his face.
"I just feel like I am to blame,

Allowing you to go with him,
Allowing him to stay here,
Allowing him to be a part of
This experience.
I'm to blame."
I take my dad and hug him tighter
Than I ever have and simply say,
"It's no one's fault but Kipp's."
It's the first time
I have ever acknowledged that.
The first.

Peter comes into the kitchen
To Dad and I hugging.
"Not again," he says
And then comes up close,
Grabs us both.
"Here's a Hulk hug."
I think my ribs might break.
"I told Mom that I threw Uncle Kipp
Across the room, and she said,
'Thank you!'"
Dad and I look at each other.
Peter continues,
"Mom said you don't have to worry.
Kipp will never bother you again.
She said that she was sorry he did those
Bad things to you, but
You will be okay now."
Peter pauses before leaving the kitchen,
Turns to our stunned looks, and adds,

"Mom also said she loves you, Dad,
And that you should go on a date."
Dad looks shocked.
I laugh and
Peter goes back to more *Star Trek*.
I say to Dad, "As hard as that sounds,
You should be open to meeting someone again.
I don't know what I would do without
Audrey's love."
Dad shakes his head.
"That won't happen, at least not anytime soon.
Your mom..." Dad pauses and leans back,
Arms over his head,
Hands clasped behind his neck.
"Your mom made life better.
I'm not sure I could ever
Hold another woman's hand again,
Or...well, anything."
I nod because I understand,
Or try to,
Realizing that I have only loved once,
And it's happening right now.
In this moment of my life,
Suddenly I feel the need
To see Audrey,
Hold her hand, as Dad had said about Mom,
And never let go.
Dad must be reading my mind.
"Go," he says.
And that's all it takes.

FIFTY-ONE

I walk toward her home
And smile as I think for a moment
That someday
I will walk toward our home
To be greeted by her eyes,
Her smell,
Taste,
Warmth.
My steps are
Rapid,
Anticipating seeing her.
Will it always be this way?
Will my heart always race
When I know
I'm getting closer to her?
I don't know the answers.
For now, I will live for her
Within the moment
And take it all in.

I arrive at her door.
Audrey's dad answers.
"She's not here."
My heart sinks.
Another question comes
To my head,

My heart.
Will I always have this
Fear,
Anxiety,
That she is okay?
But I think that's
What love is.
Loving so hard that you
Always want the other
To be safe,
Live forever
Alongside you because
The alternative is unthinkable.
"Do you know where she is?"
Her dad looks at me and says,
"Well, she said for you to come find her."
And then he smiles, and
All he needs to say is
"Go."

I find my feet on the path
Walking toward the field
And to the oak tree.
I can't stop and hug it
Because it would be taking
One more moment away from
Being with her.
The creek comes into view,
And there is Audrey,
Waiting for me

Next to the water,
Our place.

"What took you so long?" she asks.
"Well, it's a long story," I say.
"No." She pauses,
Takes my hand gently in hers,
Pulls me toward her,
And as she leans in,
Her face close to mine as
I fall into her green eyes,
She whispers, "What took you so
Long to come
Into my life and
Rescue me?"

As we lie there
Between the trees,
Below their waving branches,
With the wind on our skin,
I whisper back,
"We rescued each other."

FIFTY-TWO

There are those people,
The ones that come and find us,
Rescue us from ourselves,
And make us breathe in a little deeper,
Exhaling with a sigh from
Overwhelming love,
They are the few
Who by simply being present
Show us grace
With empathy
And allow us to take mercy on ourselves.
They can save broken spirits simply
By finding us.
I found Audrey
And she found me,
Lost somewhere
Between the trees and clouds.

FIFTY-THREE

I share this with you,
The ones that suffer
From the unbearable sorrow
Of depression,
Often caused by what you carry,
The weight that drags you down,
Making your shoulders heavy
And your mind even heavier,
Leaving you with the constant fear
Of not being able to hang on.
To you I plead,
Never let go.
For you are not alone.
You are strong.
You are resilient.
And those things that brought
Your darkness to you
Are not your fault.
They are a part of you,
Yet they are only a piece
Of your story.
Let the guilt subside,
And perhaps you too
Will find yourself,
Bringing peace
And serenity to
Quiet a wild mind.

Today is the beginning
Of a journey
Toward many tomorrows.

FIFTY-FOUR

I wake up
From a nap
Feeling dazed,
Like I'm not
In my room but
Elevated in a
Different space,
Full of confusion.
It chills me.

I look over
At packed bags
Full of old clothes,
A Yankees hat
That Dad bought me
Even though I
Hate baseball.
I start to realize
I'm in my bed,
My room,
And it will be
My last night.
Excitement
Followed by
Sadness,
Knowing that I'm
Leaving

Peter,
Leaving
Dad.

As the haziness
Of a clouded mind
Starts to clear,
Uncle Kipp
Comes into view.
I breathe
A little harder.
Being vulnerable
While asleep leads to
Trauma.
Intrusive thoughts
Start to swirl and
Come at me
All at once,
Leaving me weak
As if I can't move.

Then it happens.
Something Peter has
Been able to hear
Comes to me.
Mom's voice.
I struggle
At first, muffled,
And then she
Becomes clear.

I am
Almost frightened,
Mostly thankful,
Somewhat sad,
As hearing someone's
Voice
That is no longer here
Can bring.

"Dylan, my sweet boy,
My rolling stone."
I lie still,
Gathering my thoughts
As to what to say
To a dead mother.
"Mom, I miss you!"
She replies,
"And honey, you will
Always miss me,
And I will you."
I sit up and stare at
Nothing.
No one.
Mom continues,
"When the day is done,
You will have to accept
That I am gone,
Simply a bird that
Has flown,
A seed in the wind,

And you can see me
Whenever you close
Your eyes."

I sit on the edge
Of my bed,
Staring directly
At her picture
That I keep on my
Dresser, near me.
"I'm so scared to
Leave and live
My life." I pause.
No response.
"I'm used to having
To think about
Being raped by
Kipp and trying
To survive the
Pain.
It's like it has always
Consumed me,
Taken so much
Space in my head,
And it became my identity."
I pause,
Hoping, waiting
For a response
From a dead mother.
And then she's here

Again, telling me
What she always has.
"Dylan, my lovely boy,
You are strong, capable,
And can do whatever
You put your mind to.
I want you to live a life of
Exhaustive laughter and
Constant exploration,
Where you discover
Who you are a
Little bit at a time,
In small steps,
Because life is
Meant to be a journey."

THE LETTER

Dylan,
My beautiful boy,
On your graduation day,
As you step closer to being a man,
I offer you my words.
This life is a mystery,
A puzzle that we solve
As we try to put our pieces together
One by one,
Fitting into curved spaces.
And when the pieces don't fit,
We step back and reexamine
With curiosity
And frustration,
But when the moment comes,
And it will,
When we can see more clearly,
See life, the puzzle, for what it is,
Everything comes together,
Creating a beautiful landscape
That we worked tirelessly to create.
Do not rush your life.
Put the pieces together slowly,
One by one,
And allow the spaces
To be filled without forcing anything.
You will have a good life, my love.

I am with you in every breath.
Never forget that!
Go live your life
And trust in all its beauty.
It's there. You just have to look for it.

Love,
Mom

ACKNOWLEDGMENTS

I wrote this book for my younger self. The blue-eyed, blond-haired boy, who was often shy and reserved, a day-dreamer throughout his school days, and still is. I wrote it for the young people that are being suffocated by the trauma of being sexually assaulted and for those of us that still hold the wounds deep within our souls. Being sexually, physically, and emotionally abused as a child has forced me to bring an awareness and acceptance to the weight of carrying around these acts for over forty years. I don't believe trauma goes away. The experiences are a part of us; they shape and mold our minds, but it doesn't mean they have to ruin us. We can find peace by being gentle with ourselves, developing resilience, and not being afraid to speak up about the trauma. My goal is to halt the stigmas that society has around sexual assault and mental illness. They are not true and are only hurtful.

I also feel the need to acknowledge the strong women in my life, who have always cared for me and loved me for who I am, accepting my darkness and light. My mother-in-law, Ruth, thank you for letting me be a part of your family and your daughter's life. My mom, who has been in the battle of her life, fighting cancer, but you have always been fighting battles. You taught me resilience. Finally, I had a girl come into my life at an early age, and I can honestly say she saved me. Karen, my love, my heart, and my muse, I am not sure how our paths crossed so long ago or why I am the fortunate person to be able to love you, but I am grateful to be taking this mysterious journey called life hand in hand, by your side.

To my niece, Heather. Thank you for being one of the first readers of my book, giving honest feedback, and having the courage to look within and connect with the story.

When you grapple with the darkness of your mind, remember, there is light, it's within you, and perhaps you will find it somewhere between the trees and clouds. Breathe deep and live for the moment.

DISCUSSION QUESTIONS

1. Why did Dylan keep silent for so many years? What was he afraid of?
2. In what way is the relationship between Dylan and Peter significant?
3. What are the signs that Dylan has trauma?
4. What do you think having a friendship with Dylan would be like? How would you handle his "secret" about being sexually assaulted?
5. What are some ways Dylan has learned to cope with his trauma? What advice would you give him?
6. How is Audrey showing signs of trauma?
7. How do you define consent?
8. Should teenagers talk about sexual assault? Why or why not?
9. How can you support someone who has been sexually assaulted?
10. What are the stigmas around sexual assault? How can we combat those?

SEXUAL ASSAULT RESOURCES

RAINN (Rape, Abuse & Incest National Network)

Get confidential support from trained staff members, including having a listening ear to talk to and someone to help answer questions you might have regarding seeking medical attention, legal issues, and more.
www.rainn.org/about-national-sexual-assault-telephone-hotline
Call: 1-800-656-4673

The National Dating Abuse Hotline

Call: 866-331-9474 or 866-331-8453 (TDD)

National Suicide Prevention Lifeline

www.suicidepreventionlifeline.org
Call: 1-800-273-8255

The Society for the Prevention of Teen Suicide (SPTS)

www.sptsusu.org

National Alliance on Mental Illness (NAMI)

www.nami.org

Also by Chuck Murphree
EVERYTHING THAT MAKES US FEEL

Fifteen-year-old Neil lost his brother to suicide one year ago, and in the process, he lost his voice. Now, with his parents drifting apart and another first day at a new school, his life feels like it's spiraling out of control. That is, until Neil meets a high school counselor who gets him involved in the Polar Bear Club, where he connects with a group of classmates he can finally relate to. As their friendship grows, so do their adventures. Life throws out many challenges, and death forces us to ask "why" far too many times. In *Everything That Makes Us Feel*, Neil tries to navigate a world in search of the answers to those questions.

ABOUT CHUCK MURPHREE

by Elizabeth Ann Murphree

As Chuck's mother, I have had the privilege to watch him grow from the five-year-old little boy skipping down a soccer field instead of running, and running the wrong way on a basketball court only to make points for the opposing team. At fifteen, kicking up sod on the football field to prove he was one of the best. A picture arrived of someone I had to look at twice to recognize, wearing the United States Air Force uniform as he had changed from a boy to a man serving his country. The years went quickly. I am filled with pride at his accomplishments, which are many, a published writer now one of them. As his mother, I also find bits and pieces of his life wrapped up in the characters he writes about, their agonies and adversities. He brings all these things into his stories; I encourage you to find what I have among the pages, let them guide you into a new realm of thinking as Chuck has, as he supports young adults to embrace their need to reach out for help.

Somewhere Between the Trees and Clouds is the second novel from Chuck Murphree.

Follow Chuck on social media:
Facebook: Chuck Murphree Writer
Instagram: @chuckmurphreeauthor
Twitter: @ChuckMurphree
Spotify, Apple Podcast, Anchor: *Nothing to Prove*

www.ingramcontent.com/pod-product-compliance
Lightning Source LLC
Chambersburg PA
CBHW010814250626
47156CB00011B/3072